Rub-a-Dub-Dub

BY THE SAME AUTHOR

NOVELS

Jeremy Todd
Footsteps
Rub-a-Dub-Dub

SPORTS BOOKS [AS TEX MAULE]

The Pros (with Robert Riger)
The Game
The Players

FOR YOUNGER READERS

The Rookie
The Quarterback
Champion Quarterback
The Linebacker
The Running Back
The Corner Back
The Shortstop
Beatty of the Yankees
The Last Out

RUB-

DUB-DUB

a novel

by

Hamilton Maule

CROWN PUBLISHERS, INC., New York

Rub-a-dub-dub,
Three men in a tub,
And who do you think they be?
The butcher, the baker,
The candlestick-maker:
Turn 'em out, knaves all three!

ANONYMOUS

1

Somebody stole the watches out of the fat boy's locker while the ship was steaming down the Mississippi, bound for the Gulf of Mexico.

Next to mutiny on the high seas or fornication with a passenger, stealing ranks as the worst crime possible on board ship. There were no women on board freighters during the war, so stealing rated right up there with mutiny. Since Heavy owned the biggest share in the watch syndicate, and stood to lose the most money, he figured stealing was worse. Heavy was not a man who accepted misfortune with equanimity. He went to the captain on the bridge, and suggested that the ship be stopped forthwith and everyone on board be searched.

The captain suggested to Heavy what he could do with his watches, and sailed on down the Mississippi.

Heavy waddled painfully down to the main deck, squeezed himself into the four-to-eight fo'c's'le, and complained bitterly to Nick, who was lying in his bunk, hopefully studying French. Nick had no idea where the ship was headed, but he wanted to be prepared in case he made port in Le Havre, now that that port was secure.

He listened patiently to Heavy's outburst, and laughed.

"Serves you right," he said, "for screwing me and Mac and Stringbeans out of a hundred bucks apiece with that sad story about your poor old mother."

Heavy had bought the watches in New Orleans, hoping to sell them for a large profit in a European port. As Nick watched the fat man settle himself laboriously in his bunk, he remembered the afternoon Heavy had wheedled the money out of him.

Nick and Mac and Stringbeans were sitting in a bar called Curly Brown's on Bourbon Street down in the quarter, drinking red-eye and telling lies and waiting for Heavy to come back from the hiring hall to tell them if there were any ships on the board. They had been on the beach a couple of weeks, and still had some money left, but it was getting close to time to ship out again, and they didn't want to wait until they had to make a pierhead jump and accept anything that happened to be on the board.

Curly's was a good place for merchant marines. Nobody else came in but B girls; and as Nick sipped at his red-eye, he reflected that it was a pleasure to have a bar where he could drink comfortably without getting into a beef with the Armed Forces over not being in uniform. Most of the bars in the quarter were crowded with uniforms. Most merchant seamen did not wear uniforms; and the soldiers and sailors, once they had had enough to drink, took them for draft dodgers, and often did not stop to argue the matter.

Nick and his shipmates were a peaceable group; they did not like uniforms, and they liked trouble even less and they did like Curly and his bar. Curly had been a pretty good middleweight at one time. Looking at his mashed fighter's face, Nick thought that almost no one would take Curly for a homosexual, although he was actually as queer as a nine-dollar bill, and made no special effort to hide it. But he never propositioned his customers.

Probably doesn't bother him much at his age, anyway, Nick thought. Especially not with all the running he does.

Nick had run out of lies about how difficult it was for him to avoid the lustful advances of beautiful women in the ports of the world, and was listening to a long story by Stringbeans. Stringbeans and Mac had an advantage over him: they had been going to sea all their lives, and Nick had not shipped out until the war started, so the two of them had more material to work with.

"Hey, Nick," Curly said, interrupting Stringbeans, "hold the watch, huh?"

"Sure," Nick said, taking a stopwatch from the bartender. He felt for Curly's pulse, and found it and started the stopwatch. When it had run a minute, he stopped it.

"What was it?" Curly asked anxiously.

"Seventy," Nick said. It had actually been eighty, but he liked to make Curly feel good. Curly took his watch back and shadowboxed behind the bar, snorting through his nose the way fighters do, then shambled back off down the bar, walking with the slightly rolling, unsteady gait of a man who has been hit in the head too often. He was training for a comeback, and he thought that he would be ready if he could get his pulse down to sixty-five. He must be sixty, Nick thought. And he probably wasn't good enough when he was twenty.

"Fat boy's late," Stringbeans said. "Maybe something come up?"

"Probably another Liberty," Mac said.

Mac stretched and yawned, and tapped the bar with his glass.

"We can skip it," Nick told him. "We got another week before the draft board gets itchy."

During the war, merchant seamen were allowed a week ashore for every six weeks at sea, up to a month. Nick figured that they might stretch it a couple of days beyond, as long as they were registered at the hiring hall, since their previous trip had lasted seven months.

The afternoon was fading toward evening, and the air in the bar was a clear light amber, the color of a pale beer. It was stained by the old brown walls and the sunlight filtering through the tan canvas shade pulled down over the wide front window. Curly's place had an old bar's smell of baking bread, a smell made up of spilled beer and wine and people. Nick sniffed it appreciatively. He thought: It's a good smell if you like old bars. I do.

He waved his empty glass at Curly, and waited while Curly poured it half full of beer, then added tomato juice to fill it. He had learned to drink red-eye from Stringbeans, who said that he had picked up the habit in a Canadian port.

He watched himself drink in the back bar mirror, and thought that he was glad he had joined the merchant marine. He liked the freedom—no rank, no "sir" to say to anyone. There was variety in where he went, if not in what he did. Nick and Mac sailed as able-bodied seamen, and Stringbeans was an oiler. Heavy was an ordinary, since he was not physically capable of performing the duties of an AB.

Nick had been going to sea for nearly three years, and

now he wondered briefly if he should not put in for merchant marine officers' school. He had considered this before but had never done anything about it. For one reason or another— usually lack of money or no lack of women—he had shipped out again instead.

What the hell, he thought. I'm having fun. I bet if you could dig deep enough into the inner thoughts of most men going to war, you would find out that they liked it. I know I do, and I don't think I feel that way because all I remember is the good things like the girls and the whiskey and the bars like this one. And the irresponsibility. The danger is a part of it, and the feeling of being a member of a kind of exclusive men's club with none of the small worries of domesticity.

He looked at Mac and Stringbeans, and wondered how they felt about it. Mac had been raised on a farm in Oklahoma, but he had left home early and had been a seaman for over half of his forty years. Stringbeans was a small, thin, dark man who had been raised in the delta country of Louisiana; he was a bogalee, and he had been going to sea since he was old enough to haul his weight on a net in a shrimp boat. He sailed belowdecks, he had once told Nick, because he couldn't stand all the sunshine and fresh air on deck.

The war probably doesn't mean much to them, Nick thought. They're doing what they have always done and what they will do the rest of their lives. Nick tried to analyze why it was that he felt good, and he decided that it was because the war gave him a feeling of living for each day and not worrying about the days ahead. It was a life compressed into *now,* and because it was compressed, it was intense. The only way you can squeeze life down into so narrow a compass is to squeeze it from the time ahead, he thought. The time behind stretches back and back and grows longer and more tenuous as you move away, like the tail of a comet. But when you can be killed in the next week or day or hour, the time presses in on you and makes the *now* dense with the need for living.

"Hey, Nick," said Stringbeans, "I think you ain't too happy to go soon, eh, Nick?"

"I'm not in any hurry," Nick said. "I can wait."

"The fine ladies, they ain't in no hurry for you to go, either," Stringbeans said, laughing.

Stringbeans' last name was Boudreau, and he was a mixture of Spanish and French and whatever. Most Bogalees are fishermen, and some of them are fine jazz musicians; Stringbeans had been one and was still the other. His father had played clarinet when he was not fishing, and Stringbeans played good Dixie piano. He did not play often because he had never found a way to carry a piano in his seabag. Nick knew that he was one of the few members of the black gang who enjoyed the oily heat of the engine room. He was an indestructibly happy man, and Nick grinned at him.

"Is that bad?" he asked.

Stringbeans referred to all women as fine ladies, although most of the women he had anything to do with were neither fine nor ladies. They were B girls; they inhabited bars all over the world, not just in New Orleans. Nick wondered for a moment exactly why they were called B girls, but he did not know. They were the girls who came in and sat at the bar and hustled drinks from the customers. Most of the time their drinks were weak tea, and the customer bought them under the impression that they were whiskey and that if he could ply a B girl with enough of them he could lead her astray. Having spent enough time at Curly's to know the B girls well, Nick knew that the odds were better than even that a particular B girl was supporting a man or a widowed mother or a younger sister in a convent school. By the end of an evening spent drinking weak tea with drunks, most of them couldn't wait to get home, sit on the john long enough to dispose of the weak tea, and go to bed, alone. Some of them were vulnerable, though. They were the fine ladies Stringbeans talked about.

"Hooee, Nick," Mac said. "Ain't you about through with the Blade? And if you ain't through with her, how about Rusty?"

"Mac," Stringbeans said, with feigned sorrow. "Mac. You singing 'That Old Rugged Cross' while the band plays the funky butt blues. How long we know this Nick? Got to be two, maybe three years by now. You ever know him to give up the girl? I mean, man. Ask him for his last dollar, he say, 'You take it, man. Me, I don't need it.' Then you say, 'Hey, Nick. I see you got two girls there; gimme me one, please, man?' What does he say? 'Up yours, Maude!' That is what he say."

Stringbeans laughed and Mac shook his head and Curly walked over to see if they needed another red-eye. They did.

"Reckon you're right," Mac said. "He ain't what I would call a giving man, leastways where women is concerned. He's downright meachy. I mean, he don't let go of nothing at all. And I don't rightly know what he's got gets him so many crease, either. Tall, skinny, ugly man like that."

"He just put it in they hand, and cry," Stringbeans said, and laughed again.

Mac was as tall as Nick and uglier and skinnier. Raised on a chicken farm in Oklahoma, he left when he was seventeen because he couldn't stand cleaning out chicken batteries. He was in his forties; he had been sailing on deck ever since he deserted the chickens because he said that nothing smelled less like chicken shit than sea air. He had sparse blond hair, a mouth like a catfish, wide flat ears, and pale blue eyes that never changed expression. He was a very good gambler because of the unrevealing eyes and because he was a man of imperturbable calm. He would do anything for a friend, but Nick knew from experience that it took him a long time to decide whether you were his friend or not.

Nick grinned at them and said nothing. There was nothing for him to say; the Blade was a tall, lean, and extraordinarily passionate girl, and Rusty was shorter, plumper, and passionate enough.

Nick looked at himself in the murky mirror behind the bar, and tried to discover why he had more success with the B girls than his friends. He saw a slim man with good shoulders and chest and well-muscled arms. He was six-one and weighed 180 pounds and, since his sophomore year in college, after he had gone on a weight program, he had been reasonably proud of his build.

The face was lean and dominated by a long, high-bridged nose and sharp blue-gray eyes. The chin, Nick reflected, stuck out maybe a little too far, but not enough to mar the general effect. His hair was an indeterminate brown, and he wore it in a bristling crew cut.

The war had started when Nick was working as an insurance investigator, earning very little and bored with the tedious job of digging into the health, habits, and general insurability of from ten to fifteen applicants a day. He had joined the merchant marine thankfully; at one stroke he had found an interesting job and avoided what had been growing into an increasingly difficult entanglement with a stenographer in the office.

He had not regretted volunteering for the merchant marine. The life suited him fine. He grinned at himself in the mirror and raised his glass in a mock salute. Down with insurance investigating companies, he said to himself. Down with weepy stenographers. Down with rules and regulations and nine-to-five and the army and the navy and the coast guard, too. Up the merchant marines and, especially, up me. And the B girls, bless 'em all.

He drank the toast to himself and the good life, and held up the glass for Curly to fill. He felt good. He was twenty-eight years old, and healthy, and he had enough money for a little while more on the beach and the prospect of whiskey and B girls, and offhand he could not think of anything he needed to make him happier.

A sailor opened the door, looked in and saw the three men in civilian clothes at the bar, then closed the door and walked off down Bourbon Street. That's why this is a good bar, Nick thought.

Curly had been listening to Mac and Stringbeans talk as he washed and polished glasses, but he had not paid much attention until Mac mentioned the Blade and Rusty. Then his ears pricked up. Nick, watching him, had seen him grow alert, and thought of a dog pricking its ears, but decided the phrase did not fit Curly, whose ears resembled small potatoes. Curly's failings as a fighter were written in his face in the flat, misshapen nose and the eyebrows laced with thin worms of scar tissue. Around his mouth were threadlike white lines of old cuts. He was a tough-looking man despite his age, but Nick knew he was a gentle man. When he had to take strong measures with the drunks who started fights in his bar now and then, he hit them as kindly as possible, almost politely. He worried about his B girls.

He peered at Nick from under the ruined eyebrows that hung half over his eyes, and shook his head disapprovingly.

"You're a nice man, Nick," he said. "Why you do the way you do with them good girls?"

Nick started to deny that he had done anything to the good girls, but before he could say so, Heavy came in. He walked over to the bar and climbed ponderously on a barstool and swabbed his wet face with a sail-size handkerchief.

Watching him, Nick was surprised, as he always was, by his sheer mass. Everything about Heavy was fat except his face. He had a sharp, foxy little face set like a dimple in the middle of the fat head, almost buried by heavy, pendulous jowls and banked chins and swelling cheeks. His body was monstrous, bulging in great rolls of fat over short legs spraddled by their own girth.

He moved uncomfortably on the small barstool, his vast rump draped over it and hanging down all around. He seemed more impaled than seated on the stool, and the inadequacy of Curly's barstools never failed to irritate him.

"Soon as I find a bar with barstools built for man-sized butts, I'm leaving this crummy place," he said to Curly now. "You got barstools built for sparrow butts like Mac and Stringbeans. For a man with a real ass on him like me, they is very piercing. Gimme a brandy and sweet."

"How can you drink that stuff?" Nick said mildly. Brandy and sweet is brandy and ginger ale, a combination Nick found peculiarly sickening.

"It's better than red-eye," Heavy said. "Red-eye looks like a failing sample in a urinalysis test."

His small face was, as usual, petulant and mean. Heavy had none of the good humor of the fat man. Watching him, Nick reflected that Heavy was really a small, irascible man drowning in a sea of fat. He should have been about the size of a jockey.

"Put some ice in the glass first," Heavy said to Curly. "Then pour in the brandy over the ice, and then pour the sweet on top of that and don't stir it up like you usually do."

"I know," Curly said. "You told me maybe six thousand times."

"You still ain't got it right," Heavy said.

"You don't like it, they is other bars in the quarter,"

Curly told him. He was not angry and neither was Heavy; this exchange was a formality they went through every day when Heavy ordered his first drink.

Heavy played out the small ritual by sipping the drink suspiciously and shaking his head mournfully.

"You done it again," he said. "How can a man mix brandy and sweet and ice and come up with something tastes like horse piss?"

"Must be the ice," Curly said, and walked off down the bar.

Nick waited while Heavy sipped moodily at his drink. He wanted to ask the fat man if there were any good ships on the board, but he knew he would have to wait until Heavy had cooled off. Other merchant seamen had begun to drift in, and the sun had almost set. The bar was darker, the air now the color of bock beer. It smelled the same.

"The Liberty still the only ship up?" he asked finally.

"If they was any other, I would of told you," Heavy said testily.

"You got some special reason for the reds?" Mac asked. "Or is this just your usual case?"

Heavy twitched angrily on his barstool and started to snap back at Mac, then made an obvious effort to control himself.

"It's my old lady," he said. "She's in trouble."

Nick looked at him with surprise.

"I didn't know you were married," he said. "You never mentioned it."

"I ain't married," Heavy said. "It's my ma. She's in the clink."

"That's funny," Stringbeans said, regarding Heavy doubtfully. "Me, I didn't think you ever had a mother. Seemed to me you must of sprouted out of a wet place, like a mushroom."

"I'm serious," Heavy said. "It ain't funny when a lawyer calls you and tells you he got to have three hundred bucks to get your old lady out of jail."

"Where he call?" Stringbeans asked. "You ain't got what I would say is a permanent address."

"Called the hiring hall and left a number," Heavy said. "What worries me is I ain't got but a hundred bucks, and I need some of that to live on until we get a ship."

"What did your old lady do?" Mac asked.

"She hit a soldier in a bar in Bug Tussle," Heavy said. "He said something low-rating the merchant marines."

"You mean in Texas they put little old ladies in jail for hitting a man?" Mac asked.

"She's old but she ain't so little," Heavy said. "She weighed about three hundred last time I seen her, not more than fifty, sixty pounds' fat. The man said the soldier got a concussion, and she accidentally broke the bartender's nose on the back swing."

"So send her the money," Mac said. "Sounds like she deserves it."

"I already told you I ain't got that much," Heavy said petulantly. "How can I send what I ain't got?"

"Put the arm on Jean Baptiste," Nick suggested. Jean Baptiste was a moneylender who worked the hiring hall, and Nick knew that Heavy had borrowed from him before to finance some of his smuggling operations.

"I can't," Heavy said sadly. "I owe him from last trip for them generators I couldn't sell."

"Looks like your old lady's gonna have to do her time," Stringbeans said. "They can't give her much more than sixty days."

"The lawyer said six months," Heavy said. "And she ain't well. She's got a bad chest condition. It might be the end of her. What I was thinking was that if you all would let me have the money, I could pay it back double after the next trip."

There was a brief silence as the three seamen considered this proposition. All of them had, at one time or another, loaned Heavy money, and all of them had been repaid, after a struggle. Nick took out his wallet and checked to see how much money he had left. It came to $162 and change, and he sighed.

He counted out a hundred dollars in small bills, and handed them to Heavy.

"Here," he said reluctantly. "I wouldn't want to think of your mother in jail for six months just because I wanted to stay ashore another week."

Mac and Stringbeans contributed a hundred dollars each, even more reluctantly than Nick had, and Heavy stuffed the wad of bills into his pocket, and slid ponderously off the stool.

"I better go wire it to the man," he said. "I'll be back as soon as I can."

2

"Lay you two to one he ain't even got a mother," Mac said after Heavy had left.

Nick shook his head. He had been suspicious when Heavy started his story, but he decided that not even Heavy could dream up so unlikely a tale.

"If he had been lying, as usual," Nick said, "he would have figured out a better story. He must have been telling the truth."

"I don't know," Stringbeans said. "Seem like I remember some pretty wild stories he told when he ain't holding."

"Not about his mother," Nick said.

Two B girls came in and sat down at the bar, and Nick nodded at them.

"You buying, handsome?" one of them asked, and Nick shook his head.

"He's saving his money for Rusty," said the other one, grinning wickedly. "And I got a feeling he's gonna need it."

Nick smiled weakly and held up his empty for Curly to see.

"What does she mean?" Stringbeans asked him. "Why she gonna need it?"

"I don't know," Nick said. Curly mixed the red-eye and slid the glass down the bar with a flourish. Nick grabbed it just before it sailed off the end.

"You know," said the first B girl. "Don't he, honey?"

"Maybe not," the second one said thoughtfully. "Rusty didn't say she told him yet."

"Told him what?" Mac asked.

"It ain't for me to say," the first B girl said primly. "Them things is better told in private."

"He done it again," Stringbeans said.

"Why me?" Nick asked plaintively. "I'm not the only man ever took Rusty out."

"You the only man for the last month," the first B girl said complacently. "Least, that is what she told me."

The bar was beginning to fill up, and the two girls turned their attention to more likely prospects, to Nick's relief. He stared moodily down into his drink, doing mental arithmetic, and calculated that it was decidedly possible. While he was working this out, Heavy came back in.

"What did the lawyer say?" Mac asked him.

"Who?" Heavy said.

"The lawyer man," Stringbeans told him. "Him that was gonna get your old lady out of the bastille with our money."

"He didn't say anything," Heavy said. "I just wired him the money."

"You going to call her later and see if she got out?" Mac asked.

"She ain't got a phone," Heavy said. "She'll be okay."

"You don't seem like you're worried enough," Mac said suspiciously. "I still don't think you got a mother."

"Why should I worry?" Heavy replied philosophically. "She's out, ain't she?"

He climbed on his stool and ordered a brandy and sweet, and regarded himself in the back bar mirror with satisfaction.

"I got to admit," he said, "it makes me feel good to help my old lady."

"Look," Nick said. "I'm glad you got her out of jail, but it was us helped her. We put up the money and we'll have to ship out in a week now because of it. How about that?"

Before Heavy could reply, another voice broke in, and Nick cringed.

"You got something to take care of before you go anywhere," it said, and Nick looked around to see Rusty standing behind him.

"I got to talk to you," she said. "Right now."

Nick looked at Mac and Stringbeans helplessly, but neither of them offered help.

"Come on," Rusty said. She led him into the small room at the far end of the bar and sat down at a table. Nick sat down, gingerly, across from her.

"How are you?" he asked, and immediately wished he had not.

"Pregnant."

Nick looked at her silently, and tried to think of something apropos to say, but his mind was blank.

"You done it," Rusty said. "And you got to get it fixed."

"Fixed?"

"I know a man," Rusty said. "He does it for two hundred

dollars, and I know you got two hundred dollars. Gimme."

Nick started to reach for his pocket, then remembered Heavy's mother, and stopped.

"Look," he said desperately. "Maybe it's a mistake?"

"Not mine," Rusty said. "Where's the money?"

Nick started to tell her, and stopped.

"Well," he said at last, "you're not going to believe this."

"Try me," she said grimly. She was a pretty girl with auburn hair, and Nick had enjoyed the nights he had spent with her; but looking at her now, he wondered what he had seen in her. She's got a very mean look on her, he thought. I don't know why I never noticed it.

"I gave it to Heavy," he said. "His mother beat up a soldier in Texas and got put in jail for assault and battery, and he needed money to get her out of jail, so I let him have it."

Rusty looked at him with contempt, and laughed nastily.

"You must be hysterical," she said. "Or you think I'm some kind of a nut. I got to go right now, but I'll be back. You better come up with money or you're gonna be a husband and a father. I got friends."

She stood up and stalked away from the table, and Nick watched sadly as she left the bar. Then he got up and walked slowly back to his stool and sat down and motioned listlessly for Curly to refill his glass.

"You look like a man picked up a snake to hit a stick with," Stringbeans said. "What did she say?"

"I need my money back," Nick said to Heavy.

"You may need it," Heavy said placidly, "but you ain't gonna get it because it's already spent."

"I have to have it," Nick said doggedly. "You can get it somewhere."

"No, I can't," Heavy replied. "What do you need it for?"

"He knocked up Rusty," Mac said. "Didn't you?"

"That's what she says," Nick said. "And I believe her."

"How come you believe her?" Mac asked.

"I figured it out," Nick told him.

"I don't understand it," Heavy said bitterly. "What's Nick got?"

"Same thing you got," Stringbeans said, and laughed. "It's just easier to get to."

"Looks like a woman would want a man with meat on his bones," Heavy said. "Not a scrawny old boy like Nick."

"I need two hundred bucks," Nick said stubbornly. "She says she can get it fixed for that much."

"Don't look at me," Mac said quickly. "I gave all my extra to Heavy for his poor old mother."

"Me, too," Stringbeans said.

"Try Jean Baptiste," Heavy said. "That's what you told me to do."

"She's coming back for it in a few minutes," Nick told him. "I never saw Jean Baptiste after five o'clock in my life."

"So what is she going to do if you ain't got the money?" Mac said. "Sue you?"

"She's got friends," said Curly, who had been listening to the conversation with interest. "Take him outa here. I don't want no blood in my bar."

"Blood?" Nick asked, and shuddered.

"I seen them beat up on one or two other sailors," Curly said. "I think they may be her brothers."

"You can always marry her," Heavy said judiciously. "Might make a good wife. Then you got that fresh steak ever night, Nicky. Just go in and say, Here I am, baby. Let me have it."

"That's what she said," Nick replied. "But I'm too young to get married. I haven't lived long enough."

"It ain't so bad," Stringbeans said. "Me, I have had three. I got one working on a shrimp boat down in the bayou country right now."

"I don't want to marry a B girl anyway," Nick said.

"They're the best kind," Curly said indignantly. "The way I am, I ain't got no need for a wife, but if I was different I wouldn't have no other kind. They don't drink nothing but tea, and they got a feeling about making a man feel important and you can *talk* to them. What else do you want?"

"I don't want any wife," Nick said. "All at once you got me practically married."

He asked Curly for another drink, and stopped him as he started to mix it.

"Straight vodka on ice," he said. "I need to think."

Four vodkas later he was still thinking, and he had come no closer to a solution to his problem. Heavy was not able to give him back his money; Mac and Stringbeans had none; and Curly, whose only failing as a bartender was his absolute refusal to extend credit or loans, was no help.

Nick's thinking was becoming a little fuzzy when he made a last desperate suggestion.

"I got it," he said suddenly. "We'll sign on the Liberty tomorrow. She's almost loaded, and we'll ship right out. Who knows? We may be gone a year, and it will be all over."

"Not me," Heavy said. "Not no Liberty."

"Why not?" Nick asked. "You got me into this with your mother."

"I don't like Liberties," the fat man said. "They is too hot, too slow, too cold, and them bunks is too little."

"This is a new one," Nick said. "Maybe the new ones are different. When do they need a crew?"

"Fast as they can get one," Heavy said. "But I ain't gonna be on it."

"Wait a minute," Stringbeans said. "Me, I'm with the fat one. We ain't been on the beach long enough to make a pierhead jump. I still got two, three twenty-dollar billses the B girls ain't got out of me yet. Next week is time enough."

"How about you, Mac?" Nick asked. "Maybe just the two of us this trip. We sign now, we can get the four-to-eight."

Mac looked at him unemotionally with his pale gambler's eyes, and shook his head.

"I'll go if Heavy and Stringbeans go," he said. "We been lucky for three years. Ain't no sense in changing a winning hand."

"She can't drag you off to no preacher," Heavy said. "Nobody got to get married if he don't want to."

"He better want to," Rusty said. She was back, with friends. "Or he better come up with the money."

"I didn't say I wouldn't," Nick said.

"You didn't say you would, either," Rusty said.

"How do you know it was me?" Nick asked.

"You think I shack up with every merchant marine comes in?"

"No," Nick said. "Not every one."

When he came to, he stared dizzily up at the circle of faces above him.

"Gimme another cold beer," Mac said, and Curly handed him a stein, which he slowly and carefully poured over Nick's face. Nick spluttered and sat up, then lay back down again, painfully. He tried to remember what had happened, but his ears rang and his eyes would not focus and he had a violent, pulsing headache.

"Where did the torpedo hit?" he asked.

"He thinks he's aboard ship," Stringbeans said. "That girl got a heavy hand on her."

Nick tried to sit up again and made it, and Mac and Stringbeans hauled him to his feet and helped him onto a stool. He sat at the bar with his head in his hands, the room swinging around him in wide circles.

"Try this," Curly said, handing him a shot glass full of whiskey. Nick drank it, shuddered, and looked around him.

The bar was crowded, but no one was paying any attention to him, and he did not see Rusty and her friends.

"What happened?" he asked. "I don't remember anything."

"Rusty hit you on the head with her purse," Mac said. Nick felt his head tenderly, and discovered a lump that felt as big as a monkey fist on the back of his skull.

"Man, you got a glass skull," Stringbeans said. "Girl swats you once with a little bitty handbag, and you been out like a light for fifteen minutes. She's got a good swing, though. I got to give her that."

"It ain't the purse done it," Curly said. "Rusty has a jar of cold cream in there, so when she protects herself she got a little muscle in that bag."

Nick looked around apprehensively. "Where did she go?" he asked.

"She figured she might have killed you," Stringbeans said. "She hightailed it out of here."

"Thank God," Nick said fervently. "I couldn't take another shot like that last one."

"She must of broke the jar," Heavy said. "Next time it would be all mushy. It wouldn't hurt hardly at all."

"She probably carries a spare," Nick said. "What did she get so mad about?"

"You told her you didn't think she shacked up with *every* sailor comes in the bar," Curly told him severely. "It wasn't a polite kind of a thing to say, Nick."

"Obviously," Nick said. His eyes did not focus well, but his head felt better, and he decided the blurry vision probably came from the vodka and whiskey. Curly was at the far end of the bar, talking on the telephone. Nick waited until he had finished, then waved his glass.

"Red-eye, vodka, or whiskey?" Curly asked.

"Whiskey," Nick said recklessly.

He watched Curly pour, and asked him to put in ice and soda.

"Anyway," he said when Curly had finished, "I got to get on that boat. If she can give a man a concussion, which I think I have, her brothers will tear me limb from limb."

"Maybe not," Stringbeans said. "We can hide you somewhere."

"I'd rather go to sea," Nick said.

"I ain't riding no Liberty," Heavy told him.

"No need to decide now," Mac said. "Maybe there'll be another ship on the board in the morning."

"Maybe," Nick conceded. "We can't do anything about it tonight."

"And she ain't coming back here tonight," Stringbeans said. "Figuring she maybe killed you and all."

"That's right," Nick said. He even began to feel a bit cheerful as the whiskey slowly defeated the headache and his vision began to clear. "We'll probably get a C-2 or a Victory in the morning, and I'll never see Rusty again."

"Don't bet on it," Heavy said. "And get ready to duck."

In the mirror behind the bar, Nick saw two large, unfriendly-looking men.

3

One of the large, muscular men tapped him on the shoulder, and Nick turned around, doing his best to look innocent.

"Your name Nick?" the man asked. He looked like Rusty, with her reddish hair and a big, mean version of her face.

"No," Nick said, thinking quickly. "My name is Heavy."

"It ain't no such thing," Heavy said indignantly. "Why would anyone call a tall skinny guy like you Heavy?"

"I don't know," Nick said, laughing hollowly. "Same reason they call you Slim, I guess."

"How come someone called you Nick a while ago?" the

other man said. He was bigger than his companion, with the same rusty hair and meaner face.

"That wasn't me," Nick said. "I look like a lot of people."

The brothers looked doubtfully at each other.

"Somebody was probably talking to him," Nick said helpfully, pointing to Heavy.

"She wouldn't go for one that fat," one brother said. "She always got in trouble with skinny ones before."

"He gained a lot of weight lately," Nick said. "You wouldn't believe it."

"Must of gained a hundred pounds," Stringbeans said, entering into the spirit of the deception.

"She didn't say what he looked like," the bigger brother said. "Maybe he kind of grew on her."

"Don't hardly seem possible a man could get so hog fat so fast," the second one said. "But his name is Nick, and she said they wasn't but one Nick come in here."

"I ain't hog fat," Heavy said. "And ain't neither one of you guys gonna win any beauty prizes. You look like you been on a steady diet of ugly pills."

Mac had listened to the discussion impassively, his pale eyes wary but calm. Now he turned to Curly, behind the bar.

"Gimme a mug of beer," he said. "And give one to my friend there." He jerked his thumb toward Nick. He waited for his beer, and turned to the brothers.

"How come you all looking for Nick?" he said.

Curly drew a second beer in a heavy pewter mug and slid it down to Nick. Nick caught it as it sailed by, and thought, fleetingly, that Curly must be the worst beer and drink slider in the world. The brothers paid no attention to Mac's question.

"She said not to hurt him too bad," the big one said. "He's got to be able to pay up or stand up tomorrow."

"I ain't sure if Nick is the fat one or the tall one," the other brother said.

"You take the tall one and I'll take the fat one, then."

"Wait a minute," Heavy said in alarm. "I'm Heavy. He's Nick."

The brothers paid no more attention to him than they had to Mac. They separated slightly, and the smaller one turned toward Nick, but Nick slid off his stool and retreated around the curve of the bar. Heavy stood up and backed away from the other one; Mac and Stringbeans sat quietly, watching with interest.

"Mug of beer for me, too, Curly," Stringbeans said.

"You boys wait a minute," Mac said to the brothers. "I got a proposition for you." The brothers paused for a moment and looked at Mac. Curly drew the beer and handed it to Stringbeans, who took a long drink. From around the bar Nick watched him, and thought, A lot he cares about what happens to me.

"Since you all ain't sure which one is Nick, why don't you have a drink and wait until Rusty gets here?" Mac asked reasonably. "She can tell you which one is which."

"We ain't got time," the smaller brother said. "We got to be back on the base before too long."

"We don't mind beating up on both of them," the big one said. "It ain't hardly no trouble at all."

"Why don't you come back tomorrow?" Mac said, and drained most of his beer.

"We ain't got liberty," the big one said. He turned to his brother. "Johnny, I'm gonna git mine now. You hit yours."

He moved suddenly, and Heavy, acting with the surprising speed of some fat men, skipped away from him, taking shelter behind Mac. Nick backed farther away from the other brother, who was stalking him.

As the big one, after Heavy, went by Mac, Mac hit him carefully on the top of the head with the heavy pewter mug. The blow made a sound like the deep ring of a large bell, and the big brother staggered briefly.

The littler brother looked around, and Nick swept his beer off the bar and hit him, forgetting that the stein was full, and spraying beer liberally over the customers, who were watching with fascination. The smaller brother staggered too, but Nick noticed that his blow did not ring as true as Mac's had. It must have been the beer in the stein, he thought.

The big brother had recovered and now was chasing Mac into the small back room, clearing a wide path through the customers. Seeing that his adversary was still groggy, Nick ran after them and fetched the big brother a hard blow on the back of the head, distracting him momentarily.

"Hit the other one; he's getting up again," he heard Stringbeans yell, and looked around to find Stringbeans perched safely on top of the bar and the younger brother coming toward him. Nick circled warily as the man advanced and backed him against the bar. He was watching Nick when Stringbeans drove him to his knees with a full-arm swing with a beer mug he had commandeered from Curly.

Nick heard another hollow *bong* just behind him, and turned in time to see that Mac had scored on the big one, who had sneaked up behind Nick. This blow dropped him to his hands and knees, and Nick thought the battle was over until he heard Heavy yell, "The other one's getting up again!"

He turned in time to ward off a charge by the younger brother, catching him on the side of the head with the beer mug as he went by. He staggered slightly but went on toward Mac, and Nick ran after him and hit him again on the back of the head. The beer mug no longer rang with a clear bell tone. Nick looked at it, and found that it had been battered out of shape.

The bigger brother was getting up now, and Nick hit him again, wondering how long this was going to go on. He was beginning to get arm weary. As he leaned against the bar and saw Mac drop the little one, Stringbeans, squatting on the bar behind him, said, conversationally: "Kick him in the balls. Bastard's got a cement head."

"Sit on him," Nick said to Heavy as he turned to go to Mac's aid again; Heavy had been leaning against the bar, avoiding action. This time he and Mac attacked together and flattened the remaining brother. Nick rested wearily against the bar and looked back to see if Heavy had cooperated. Heavy was sitting placidly on the head of the smaller one, who was kicking feebly.

Nick was breathing heavily. His legs were tired and his mouth was dry, and he had forgotten the flattened mug in his hand until the larger brother twitched and tried to climb to his feet again. Nick rapped him smartly on the forehead, and he subsided.

"You want me to get off this one?" Heavy asked, and Nick walked wearily down the bar to inspect Heavy's captive. He had quit moving by now.

"Better get him off," Stringbeans said. He had climbed down from the bar. "Can't be very healthy for that man with Heavy sitting on his head like a nesting hen. May have mashed it flat."

"It don't feel flat," Heavy said complacently. "He made a few snuffly noises a while back, but he been real quiet lately."

"Get up," Nick said. "Hurry. You probably suffocated the poor bastard."

Heavy climbed laboriously to his feet, and all of them looked down at the smaller brother, who lay perfectly still.

"Took three of you to handle the other one," Heavy said proudly. "I didn't need no help at all with this one."

"Feel his pulse," Curly said from behind the bar. "Wait until I get the stopwatch."

"He's still warm," Nick said, feeling the forehead of the unconscious man. "May even have a little fever."

He took the stopwatch from Curly and found the man's

pulse and counted silently for sixty seconds, then shook his head doubtfully.

"It's a little over a hundred," he said.

"You think he's hurt bad?" Heavy asked. His little face was worried. "I didn't do it. It was you guys hit him on the head. I just sat on him."

"You all better get out of here," Curly said. "We'll drag them out on the street, and ain't nobody can prove it happened in here."

"How about him?" Mac said, pointing to the bigger brother.

"It's my word against his," Curly said. "And I got a little juice in the precinct."

They hauled the two brothers into the deserted street and left them there. Then they went back into the bar, and Curly fixed red-eye for Mac and Stringbeans and Nick and a brandy and sweet for Heavy.

They sipped silently for a moment; then Heavy said. "Maybe we better get on that Liberty after all."

"I'm ready," Nick said. "Right now."

"Not me," Stringbeans said. "I ain't never shipped when I had any twenty-dollar bills, and I still got a few."

"Spend 'em tonight," Heavy said. "I ain't gonna stick around here and wait to get arrested."

They argued for a few moments before they could convince Stringbeans. He agreed only when he saw a police car slow down and stop in front of the bar. The four seamen went out the back door hurriedly and spent the rest of the night using up their money on B girls and bad whiskey in other bars.

4

When they reached the hiring hall the next morning, the Liberty ship was the only one on the board. It was hot and still in the dingy room, and a few seamen were sitting at the tables playing cards.

"Let's wait a little," Nick said. "Maybe a C-2 or a Victory will come up." They waited until early afternoon, but the board was unchanged, and finally Heavy said, nervously: "We better sign on. No telling when the cops gonna come in here looking for us."

"Okay," Nick said. "Let's put our cards in."

They turned in their cards, received shipping slips, and left the hall. They walked through the quarter, heading for the commissioner's office to sign on, going slowly to accommodate themselves to Heavy's waddle. The fat man stopped outside a small jewelry store.

"I gotta pick up my watch," he said. "It's being fixed. I hope it's ready."

"It's on your wrist," Nick said.

"Not this one," Heavy said. "I got another one. You all go on, and I'll meet you at the commissioner's office."

They walked on, and Heavy ducked into the jewelry shop.

The signing on was quick, and Heavy arrived just as Nick finished his papers.

"What took you so long?" Mac asked him.

"It wasn't quite ready," Heavy said. "I had to wait a little while. I didn't want to leave it because my old lady gave it to me."

He signed his papers quickly, and they walked to the small seamen's hotel where they had left their gear. They picked up their seabags, and Heavy carried a big paper carton under his arm. They hailed a cab to take them to the dock.

"What's in the box?" Nick asked Heavy. "You didn't have it yesterday."

"My watch," Heavy said shortly.

"In a box that big?"

"I wanted lots of padding around it," Heavy said.

They reached the docks quickly and struggled up the gangplank. As they came aboard, Nick noticed that the ship was loaded, with steam on deck; she would be moving out into the stream shortly, for a tug was already standing by.

Heavy dropped his seabag on the deck and looked back down at the dock.

"Damn if I ever thought I'd be happy to sail on a Liberty again," he said. "But I sure as hell am. You suppose that guy got all right?"

"I doubt it," Mac said, grinning his catfish grin. "But it ain't your worry now."

"I hope Rusty makes out all right," Nick said, feeling a twinge of guilt.

"A fine lady like her is going to find someone else to take your place," Stringbeans said philosophically. "Let's find a fo'c's'le."

They made their way into the midship house, and Stringbeans left them to go below and find the first assistant engineer and discover which watch he was on. Nick, Heavy, and Stringbeans walked down the hot, narrow companionway peering into fo'c's'les until they found a vacant one, where they dropped their seabags on the empty bunks. All the other fo'c's'les had gear in them already, although the deck gang was topside and the small rooms empty of seamen.

"They must of made up watches already," Mac said. "You want the top bunk, Nick?"

The fo'c's'le had two bunks below and one above, and Nick heaved his seabag onto the top one. He knew that Mac preferred a lower bunk, and it was impossible for Heavy to climb into the upper, as well as being dangerous for the man below him.

"Okay," Nick said. He began to open his seabag, and pulled out some work gear. "Looks like all hands are turned to. We better get out on deck."

They changed into dungarees and walked forward. The deck gang was busy cradling the booms on the Number One hatch as Nick followed Mac and Heavy forward along the cluttered deck. As they reached the hatch, a short, slight young man with a blond crew cut stopped them.

"You the two AB's and the ordinary?" he asked, and Nick nodded.

"We just came aboard," he said. "Watches made up?"

"You're on my watch," the young man said. "I'm Mr. Fitch. The chief mate."

"The four-to-eight," Mac said with satisfaction. "Good."

The three seamen looked at the young first mate curiously. Probably first trip as a chief, Nick thought. The mate looked back at them for a moment, then ducked his head and looked away. He seemed unsure of himself, and Nick felt sure now that he was sailing chief for the first time.

"You fellows better turn to," the mate said now. "The bosun is over there. He'll tell you what to do."

"Aye, aye," Nick said. "He the old bald-headed one?"

The first looked over at the short, pudgy, bleary-eyed man Nick had indicated and studied him for a moment, as if trying to justify Nick's description. Finally, he nodded. "Yes," he said. "That's him."

He was silent again for a moment, studying the deck uncomfortably, and Nick looked down to see if there were something there. The deck was littered, but beneath the usual debris of a sailing day it was clean and freshly painted, and Nick recalled with a brief pleasure that the ship had come new from the shipyards. There should not be much chipping and scraping and painting, he thought to himself.

The mate looked up at last, and smiled.

"I hope we'll have a good watch," he said. "This is my first trip as a chief mate."

The three seamen looked at the mate noncommittally before Nick smiled at him. He could see that the young mate was uncomfortable and unsure of himself, and he wanted to help if he could.

"We'll get along," he said. "You probably have more sailing time than all of us put together."

The mate ducked his head shyly again, and walked away aft. Heavy watched him go, his small face puckered in disgust.

"Now we got a snotnose for a first," he said to the others. "Got to wet-nurse him, I expect."

"Seemed all right to me," Mac said mildly.

"We got the four-to-eight, anyway," Nick said. "I figured

coming on board last, we'd get stuck with the twelve-to-four."

"Probably all boots on the other watches," Mac said. Sailors on the chief mate's watch worked from four to eight in the morning and the same hours in the evening, and usually earned a good deal more overtime than the other watches and did far less work on deck when the ship was under regular watches at sea. By union rules, seamen could work on deck only between the hours of eight in the morning and five in the afternoon, during their watches. This left only one hour for members of the four-to-eight to work without being paid overtime, from four to five on the afternoon watch. Since two members of the watch were engaged either on the wheel or on lookout, it meant in effect that Nick would perform deck work only once every three days, if the mate allowed Heavy to steer. Since ordinary seamen were usually allowed to steer during the war, Nick felt reasonably sure that Fitch would not object to Heavy taking a wheel watch.

"We better check in with Boats," Nick said, leading the way across the deck toward the small, untidy-looking man the mate had pointed out.

Nick told the bosun who they were, and he blinked at them through squinting, watery blue eyes.

"Any one of you all ever been to thea before?" He sprayed Heavy, who was closest to him, with a gentle fog of spittle as he lisped. He was toothless as well as bald.

"The whole watch been to sea," Mac said while Heavy brushed himself off angrily.

"AB's got AB papers?"

"Both of us," Nick said. "Him and me." He indicated Mac by a jerk of his head. "Heavy is the ordinary."

"One of you is got to take the wheel," the bosun said. "Other AB's is all acting, just got out of school. Couldn't steer a dinghy in a bathtub."

"You take it," Mac said to Nick. "I'll relieve you in a couple of hours."

"Okay," Nick agreed. It would not make much difference who took the wheel first. From the condition of the hatches and booms and the litter on the deck, Nick figured the deck gang would be working all night, anyway.

When he reached the flying bridge, Nick relieved the third mate, who had been standing by the wheel, ready to take the wheel watch, if necessary, because the pilot had refused to work the ship in the river with a boot on the wheel.

The deck gang was taking in the lines as Nick took over. He was not happy about steering a new ship down the Mississippi, but there was nothing he could do about it. He knew it would take time for him to grow accustomed to the special qualities of the *Andrew Crichton*. He looked down to the deck and watched the deck gang cradling booms, and decided he was probably better off on the wheel after all. They were working uncertainly and clumsily under the profane direction of the bosun, and Nick hoped that Mac would take his time about coming up to relieve him. It was easier and a good deal safer on the flying bridge.

He stole a glance at the pilot, an erect old man with a short white beard, then looked forward at the broad muddy river beginning to slip under the bow of the Liberty. The tug had cast off its lines, and the ship was moving under its own power and Nick's control.

"Port easy," the pilot said, and after a momentary hesitation, Nick spun the wheel gently. As the *Andrew Crichton* hesitated, Nick put on more wheel, and she began to swing quickly. It was nearly an hour before Nick had learned some of her more obvious idiosyncrasies and could judge accurately how much wheel she took to meet the wheel commands.

Like all Liberties, she was named after a merchant seaman who had been killed in action. Later, Nick found out that

Andrew Crichton, for whom this Liberty was named, had sold his papers to his brother-in-law and spent the war on a chicken farm in South Texas.

Nick might have mastered the peculiarities of the *Crichton* in less than an hour if the pilot had not been an old-timer. Pilots were supposed to use left and right in giving commands, instead of the traditional port and starboard, in deference to the flood of boots who sailed during the war. This pilot either had never heard of the rule or chose to ignore it.

On the first wheel command, when the pilot said "Port easy," Nick was startled. Port is short and left is short, so he means left, he said to himself and began to give the ship the left wheel.

"Smartly there, Quartermaster!" the pilot barked.

"Aye, aye, sir!" Nick replied, and spun the wheel faster.

"And repeat the wheel command when I give it to you," the old man said. He was tough and crusty, but Nick realized very soon that he was an excellent pilot.

The bow of the *Andrew Crichton* was swinging at an alarming rate now, and for a moment Nick was afraid that they would wind up headed away from the Gulf, toward St. Louis.

"Meet her!" the pilot said, calmly enough, and Nick spun the wheel the other way.

"Meet her it is," he answered, and felt very nautical. He would not have known the proper reply if he had not read some of C. S. Forester's Horatio Hornblower novels on previous trips. For two years he had followed instructions promptly on the bridge, but the wartime merchant marine officers he had sailed under had not bothered with formalities.

"Steady as she goes," the pilot said over his shoulder, studying the face of the river.

"Steady it is," Nick answered. The pilot looked back at him with approval, and Nick did his best to impersonate an old salt. He peered keenly ahead, trying to decide if the bow was still swinging or if it was steady. It was hard for him to tell, but the pilot seemed satisfied, so Nick left the wheel amidships, hopefully.

They were sailing down one of the rare long straight stretches of the river, and the pilot relaxed. He seemed to have decided that Nick really was an old hand. Nick, busy aiming the ship at a distant tall tree as carefully as he could, was surprised when the old man spoke to him.

"Seems to be a yar ship," the old man said.

"Never steered one as yar," Nick answered, wondering what "yar" meant. "She's trimmed a little too much down by the stern," the pilot said.

"Seems to be, sir," Nick said judiciously. He wondered what had been taken off the back of the ship.

"Probably be a little difficult to steer in a quartering sea," the pilot went on.

"Just what I was thinking, sir," Nick replied. He wished he had given more attention to the nautical parts of the Hornblower novels.

"You're holding a fine course, lad," the pilot said. "Steady as a rock and true as an arrow."

"Thank you, sir," Nick said.

"You mind standing a double wheel watch?" the pilot asked him. "The river gets tricky on down a way."

Nick looked down on the foredeck and watched Heavy hammering in chocks as he worked on battening down the Number Two hatch. Thinking that he would much rather be on the wheel than working in the wet heat on deck, he said, quickly, "Not at all, sir."

The ship's captain was standing on the wing of the bridge, and the pilot walked over to him.

"We get too many ninety-day wonders these days," he said to the captain. "This lad seems to be a fine, alert quartermaster. I'll wager he has been going to sea all of his life. He's got the look of a seaman. Right, Quartermaster?"

"Aye, aye, sir," Nick said cleverly. Heavy and Mac were now hauling steel cross-battens over the hatch covering on Number Three, sweating copiously, and Nick could hear the bosun cursing at the boots who were still trying to get the chocks in on Number Two. "Since I was fourteen, sir," Nick added.

"How old are you now?" the pilot asked.

"Twenty-seven, sir," Nick said, telling the truth for the first time.

"Should have taken your mate's papers by now," the pilot said reprovingly.

"I've got third mate's papers," Nick said. He had barely passed his examination for able-bodied seaman.

The pilot looked back at the river, and yelled, "Hard astarboard!"

Nick thought starboard is long and right is long, so he must mean to turn right, and he spun the wheel hard to the right. He had forgotten to keep the ship aimed at the tall tree during his conversation with the pilot, and by the time the *Andrew Crichton* began to take the wheel, he saw a rice plantation only a point off the port bow, and closing fast.

I should have let Mac take the wheel, Nick thought sadly. He wondered what would happen when the ship went aground, and braced himself for the shock.

5

The *Andrew Crichton*'s peculiarity of answering the wheel very quickly when it did answer was the only thing that saved Nick and the ship. Nick had closed his eyes in despair, and two Negro field hands working in the rice paddy at the river's edge were fleeing inland in twin clouds of spray when the bow swung away from the shore and toward the middle of the river again. Feeling no shock of collision with the shore, Nick opened his eyes and breathed a gusty sigh of relief.

The pilot and the captain were standing side by side, gripping the bridge rail. They look very tense, Nick thought apprehensively.

When it became clear that the ship had swung far enough

out into the stream to make sure that it would not run aground, the captain and pilot turned together and regarded Nick, who tried to appear unconcerned.

"Very tricky currents along here," he said. "Especially when she is trimmed down by the stern, sir."

The pilot let go of the rail and took his cap and rubbed his hand through his mane of white hair.

"Port easy," he said in a carefully restrained voice.

"Port easy it is," Nick answered. No one said anything after that.

Nick was busy at the wheel for a time. The Mississippi is a wide river from New Orleans to the Gulf of Mexico, he thought, but it can't make up its mind which way it wants to go to get there. Nick managed to avoid the banks for the rest of his wheel watch. When an acting AB from the eight-to-twelve came up to relieve him in the early dusk, he was thankful. He noticed that the pilot did not seem to feel any great sorrow in losing him.

He probably doesn't really believe I have been going to sea since I was fourteen, Nick thought as he left the flying bridge. Probably doesn't believe I have a third mate's license either. Nick felt sorry about that.

It was almost dark as he went below, and the deck gang had knocked off for dinner. Nick went into the crew's mess to join them, and found that he was suddenly very hungry.

He looked forward with some hope and considerable trepidation to his first meal on the *Andrew Crichton*, since he would be living on the same fare for an uncertain length of time. Next to having a good first mate and a good bosun, he liked most having a generous steward and a reasonably competent chief cook.

Mac and Heavy and the rest of the deck gang, with most of the engine-room crew, were already seated when Nick entered the crew's mess.

"Boats knock off the deck gang early?" he asked as he sat down at the long table. Mac shook his head.

"Nope," he said. "He disappeared a couple hours ago. Must of had a bottle stashed somewhere. Probably in the paint locker, because he spent a lot of time checking it, and we damn sure weren't painting anything. Finally he started singing and then he danced a little bit, and the last we saw of him he was headed for the midship house talking to himself. I looked in his fo'c's'le a little while ago, and he was passed out."

"Who worked the deck gang?" Nick asked.

"The chief," Mac told him.

"How is he?"

"Seems like a pretty good head," Mac said.

"He's a good head all right," Heavy said morosely. His big body was crammed uncomfortably into one of the chairs fixed to the deck alongside the table, and his little face peered out of the fat head malevolently. "Kind of head I'd like to stuff and put up over the mantelpiece."

"He knocked us off ten minutes early," Mac said mildly.

"He figured he better before one of those nuts dropped a boom on him," Heavy said. "He's just like every other first mate."

He grunted disdainfully and waved at the messboy, who was at the other table. Heavy did not like first mates, and Nick understood. First mates did not like Heavy. He was more of a passenger than a seaman, because of his size. He could not go aloft at all; if he had to climb to the top of a mast house, it took him ten minutes to struggle up the short ladder, and after he had reached the top he had to rest for half an hour.

"What did the first do to you?" Nick asked.

"Wanted me to go up the Number Two mast and secure an Irish pennant," Heavy said bitterly. "I told him ordinaries don't got to go aloft. He said ordinaries on *his* watch go aloft, and I say, 'Mr. Mate, you go talk to the deck delegate and see what the union rules say about that.' "

"We ain't elected a deck delegate yet," Mac said.

"I know that, man," Heavy told him. "I figured it to take him a long time to find a deck delegate when we ain't got one. But then he look right at me and he say: 'Maybe you are right, fat boy. If you was to go aloft, it might tip the whole ship over. So get you a sledge and knock in the chocks on the hatches.' So I been swinging a sledge the whole watch."

"You got three hours' overtime," Nick said unfeelingly. "Just like Mac. Me, I didn't get any overtime standing a wheel watch."

"Next time I'll take the wheel watch," Heavy said. "My arms is so sore I can't comb my hair."

"Ain't no need to," Stringbeans said. He had just come in, so Nick knew he had the four-to-eight watch below. "Ain't no fine ladies aboard the *Andrew Crichton*." He cast a speculative eye at the messboy serving at the other table, and grinned. "Ain't even no pretty messboys."

"You can't stand a wheel watch anyway," Nick said. "You ever hear of an ordinary taking the wheel on the Mississippi? You have to have experience as a quartermaster before a river pilot will let you take the wheel."

"Like you?" Heavy said, and snorted. "You left a wake like a snake. Man, I dropped my sledge and headed for the lifeboats one time there. We was working on Number One and I look up and I could of shook hands with a man working in a rice field except he was too busy running. You got to be the worst driver I ever saw, man."

"It was the pilot's fault," Nick said. "You want me to turn the ship without him telling me to?"

"That would be all right with me," Heavy said. "I ain't very anxious to wind up in the middle of a rice plantation."

He turned to look for the messboy again just as the bosun wobbled in. Nick studied him as he stood in the doorway. He had not had time to look him over very carefully on the deck; now he saw that the old man was even more disreputable than he had appeared at first glance.

He looked to be at least seventy years old, and Nick thought that he must have spent the last twenty of those under three feet of stagnant water. His head was as bald as a bollard, and his scalp was a mottled, scaly pinkish brown. He stood weaving gently in the doorway, peering into the room through eyes that resembled small blobs of pink Jell-O. His nose was long and thick and so pendulous its tip nearly touched a chin that curled up to meet it over the toothless wreck of a mouth.

As the bosun swayed in the doorway, blearily surveying the crew, the messboy came in from the galley with plates of food, and the bosun watched him mistily for a moment.

"Meshboy," he said, "I'm the boshun on thish ship, and I mesh before anyone else and don't you forget that."

The messboy looked at him uncertainly, then put the plates down on the tables in front of the seamen who had ordered them. As Nick watched him, he thought that he looked like a farm boy fresh from the cornfields of Iowa. He was very young and pimply and nervous, and Nick surmised that he had never sailed before. He was watching the bosun apprehensively now, and obviously did not know what to do about the unprovoked attack.

The bosun had tottered all the way into the messroom, and the messboy watched him warily. He tried to edge by the bosun to return to the galley for more orders, and the bosun picked up a coffee mug from a mess table and tried to hit him with it. He missed widely.

"Man couldn't hit his butt with both hands," Stringbeans said.

The messboy fled into the galley, and the bosun looked around defiantly.

"Ain't he a beauty?" Heavy asked in disgust.

"Looks like a long trip," Mac said. "For the messboy, anyway."

The bosun wandered around aimlessly for a few moments and finally collapsed into a seat across the table from Heavy. He looked around at the seamen near him, staring at one after the other, then smiled. Nick watched him in fascination; when he smiled, the toothless gums and the rubbery lips made him look as if he had two sets of lips.

"I been shailing forty-odd year," the bosun announced to the room at large. "And I never saw such a loushy-looking deck gang in my whole life."

He had fastened his eyes on Stringbeans as he said this, and Stringbeans looked at him in surprise.

"I don't sail on deck, you toothless old bastard," he said mildly.

"Oh, sho it'sh come to that already," the bosun said indignantly. "We ain't dropped the pilot yet, and it'sh mutiny on the high sheas!"

"We're still in the river," Nick pointed out.

The messboy came back in from the galley and gave one of the AB's from the eight-to-twelve his plate. He stood well out of arms' reach from the bosun, and asked him, timidly, "What would you like, sir?"

The bosun gave up trying to stare Stringbeans down and turned to the messboy.

"Shteak," he said. "A *tender* shteak, boy. And get the lead out of your butt or I'll have you keelhauled."

"Jesus," Stringbeans said, "this man thinks he's sailing with John Paul Jones."

"I ain't forgot you," the bosun said. "Scrawny black-headed bastards like you is always troublemakers. I mind twenty year ago—"

"Can it," Stringbeans said. "I'm an oiler. I don't got to take no crap from you, Bosun. And I'm glad I'm not a deck-hand with a fruitcake like you sailing boats."

"I'm the boshun," the old man said vaguely. "If you can whip the boshun, you can have hish job. And ain't no shon of a bitch ever shailed the sheven sheas can whip this bosun."

When he said "shailed the sheven sheas" he sprayed Heavy, sitting across the table, with a dense mist. Heavy, who had been devoting himself silently to disposing of his steak so he could eat another, slammed his knife and fork down on the table with a bang.

"Spray the other way, you old bastard!" he yelled. "You done ruined my dinner." He mopped himself with his napkin, and Nick could see from the color of his face that he was growing angrier. When he had dried himself as well as he could, he leaned across the table as far as possible and tried earnestly to stuff the napkin in the bosun's mouth.

The bosun stood up to avoid Heavy, glared back at him, then looked around the crew's messroom. He was about five feet four inches tall, and Nick thought he would have trouble whipping the messboy, who was even smaller.

"It'sh a conspiracy," the bosun said, waving his fists. "One at a time or in watches or all at once. Come on."

The seamen at the tables looked at him and grinned, and turned back to their food. No one offered to meet his challenge.

"Sit down," Mac said to him. "If anybody wants to whip the bosun, he's got to do it ashore. They put you in the clink if you try it at sea."

The old man stayed up defiantly for another moment, but no one was paying any attention to him and he sat down again when the messboy approached with his food.

Nick was nearly through with his own steak by now, and had found, to his satisfaction, that it was at least edible, if a bit tough. The food at the beginning of a trip or just out of any port was usually better than at any other time, since the vegetables were fresh and the meat had not been frozen long enough to lose its taste. Nick asked the messboy for fresh coffee, and watched the bosun curiously, wondering how he would attack the steak without the benefit of teeth.

Most of the rest of the crew had finished eating, too, and the messboy was kept busy for a while serving coffee. By the time he was finished, most of the hands had turned their attention back to the bosun, who had begun his attack on the meat.

He tried at first to cut it into small bites, but his hands were too unsteady and the knife was not sharp enough. He gave up at last and picked the steak up in both hands. He gummed it as hard as he could for a minute or two, but as far as Nick could tell, he didn't make an appreciable dent in it.

He changed grips and tried another part of the steak, with no better luck, and put the steak back in his plate to consider another plan of attack. By now the room was quiet as the crew watched the struggle. The bosun ate a few bites of mashed potatoes before he realized that he had become the center of attention.

"What'sh everybody looking at?" he asked through a mouthful of mashed potatoes, with disastrous results for Heavy.

Heavy, pinned in place by his chair and the pressure of the edge of the table on his big belly, was helpless to avoid the potato shower. He turned red with rage, the heavy flaps of his jowls trembling in his agitation.

"I'm gonna kill him!" he howled, struggling to get up. "So help me God, I'm gonna murder him!"

"Didn't you guys never see a man eat a shteak before?" the bosun asked, paying no attention to Heavy.

The messboy came in with Heavy's second steak, and the fat man quit trying to get up and dabbed at himself with his napkin. He glared at the bosun again, but the fragrance of the steak was too much, and he slowly subsided.

"I'm gonna wear my foul-weather gear if that old bastard ever sits across from me again," he said bitterly before he started to eat.

"You ain't bit that steak hard enough to make a baby holler yet," Stringbeans said to the bosun. "If the steak had teeth, it would of ate you up by now."

"I got teeth," the bosun said with dignity. "They ish right here in my pocket." He reached in his shirt pocket and triumphantly produced a set of false teeth.

"I got a idea," Stringbeans said, grinning. "Put the steak in your pocket with the teeth, and I'll bet you two to one on the steak."

"It ain't no better than a even bet," Mac said. "Maybe six to five."

"You and me ish goin' to the captain," the bosun said to Stringbeans. "Thish is the shecond time you inshulted me."

"Put your teeth in," Mac said to him. "Then see can you eat the steak." Mac turned to Nick and said, seriously, "I'll lay you five bucks he can't get a bite off it."

"No bet," Nick said. "But I'd like to see him try."

The bosun put his teeth in his mouth, but it did not notably improve his appearance. To Nick, it looked as if the teeth must be at least two sizes too big, if teeth came in sizes like shoes or hats. The bosun tried to say something to Mac, but he lost control of the loose teeth and they bit him sharply on the lower lip. After extricating his lip with some difficulty, he pushed the teeth farther into his mouth and picked the steak up again.

This time he got a firm two-handed hold on the steak. The room was so quiet that Nick could hear the clatter of dishes in the galley as the messboys worked at cleaning up. The bosun opened his mouth carefully, controlling the teeth well, fitted the steak between the uppers and lowers, and settled it in place and then bit down as hard as he could.

He looked around triumphantly at the watching crew, and gnawed industriously for a long minute. He did not appear to be making much progress, and Nick watched as he rested for a few seconds, then tried again. He had no better luck the second time.

"I'll lay five to one on the steak," Mac said. "Up to five bucks."

There were no takers, and the bosun tried to disengage himself from the steak. He opened his mouth wide, but the teeth stayed stuck in the steak; finally he removed the steak, complete with teeth.

He put it on his plate, pried the teeth loose with his knife, and put them back in his shirt pocket. No one said anything. Nick looked at the steak and saw that it had a clearly discernible set of tooth marks in it.

"He might have won if he had been in shape," Nick said to Mac. "He just didn't have enough left for the stretch."

"Here he goes again," Mac said, and Nick turned back to watch.

The bosun had come to grips with the steak again, this time without the teeth. He was holding the steak close before his face, studying it with his watery pink eyes, and finally he set his gums approximately in the tooth marks and gummed it vigorously, shaking his head from side to side. To Nick he looked like a puppy worrying a shoe.

"Twenty to one," Mac said hopefully, and looked around.

The bosun tired quickly this time, and returned the steak to his plate with what Nick thought was a touch of sorrow.

"This is a very tough piece of shteak," he said. "Who is the deck delegate?"

"We ain't picked one yet," Mac told him. "Anybody here ever been a deck delegate?"

Since all the deck crew with the exception of Nick, Mac, and Heavy were making their first trip, it was a rhetorical question. Nick figured they were all on trip cards—permits issued to nonunion members to make their first trip, without voting privileges in union meetings. He doubted that most of them knew what a deck delegate was; so far as he could remember, the training course at the merchant marine school in St. Petersburg had not included an explanation of the workings of the seamen's unions.

A middle-aged man with graying hair and a small potbelly who had watched the proceedings quietly asked, diffidently, "What is a deck delegate?"

The bosun snorted in disgust, and Nick answered.

"The deck delegate represents the deckhands in any arguments with the captain or the shipping company over union matters," Nick said. The man nodded and turned back to his coffee. He looked as if he should be a bookkeeper in an insurance office, and Nick wondered what had possessed him to go to sea.

"How much does he get paid?" another deckhand asked, this one looking even younger than the messboy, but a big, strong youngster who would have seemed at home as a fullback on a high school football team.

"Nothing," Nick told him. He had sailed deck delegate once. "All he gets is headaches. A lot of them."

"How come anyone wants the job, then?" the youngster asked. Nick decided he had joined the merchant marine from a sense of adventure or because he could not get into the Armed Forces for some reason.

"No one wants it," he said. "But someone has to take it.

The crew picks the delegate. Only union members are allowed to vote."

"That means they is just three of us voting," Heavy said. "The trip cards ain't got a voice, and the bosun can't vote because he's the bosun. So that just leaves me and you and Mac, Nick."

"I nominate Nick," Mac said quickly.

"I second him," Heavy said before Nick could protest.

"All in favor say 'Aye,' " Mac went on, and he and Heavy drowned out Nick's anguished cry of "No!" with resounding "Ayes!"

"Looks like you the deck delegate," Stringbeans said sympathetically. He could afford to be sympathetic, since the black gang had elected their delegate before he had come aboard. "Good luck."

"I'm going to need it," Nick said gloomily.

6

Nick's problems began at once.

"Since you're the deck delegate, you go tell the old man they ain't gonna be no feeding out of two potsh on thish ship," the bosun said to Nick as soon as the election was over. I bet they ain't feeding horshe meat like thish in the saloon mesh."

"Tomorrow night," Nick said unhappily. "If the meat is the same tomorrow night, I'll go see the skipper at dinnertime so I can see what they are eating in the officers' mess."

Everyone but the bosun agreed to this. The bosun grumbled for a while, then sent his gnawed steak back to the galley and asked for another one, and the chief cook came out to see who was complaining about the food.

Like most chief cooks, he was a fat man, not as fat as

Heavy but not far from it. He listened to the bosun's complaint with reasonable good nature.

"I don' mek you another steak, mon," he said finally, speaking with what Nick recognized as a West Indian accent. "I do, you go loose yo' tempah again. Two poached eggs I fix, mon. Tendah so you can bite dem."

He went back to the galley, and the bosun looked at Nick.

"You heard that, Mr. Delegate," he said, and Nick nodded.

"A man's got the right to eat meat," the bosun said. "The chief cook won't give it to him, that'sh cause for charges. You make a note. I'm bringing the cook up on charges next union meeting I make after we reach port."

The cook came back with the poached eggs and gave them to the bosun, laughing.

"Okay, mon," he said. "An' I going to be there, also. And you going to have to eat the steak I cook, right there in de meeting."

The bosun found nothing to say to that. Nick watch him wolf down the poached eggs and the mashed potatoes, and could not help feeling sorry for the old man. When the bosun finished, he made his way out of the messroom, and Nick could hear him grumbling to himself as he walked down the companionway toward his fo'c's'le.

The chief mate looked in and said, "Watch below turn to aft to cradle booms and secure hatches." Nick sighed and got up.

"Long night ahead," he said. "I hope he knocks us off time enough to get a little sleep before we go on watch."

The mate let the four-to-eight off at midnight, and it was when Mac and Heavy and Nick returned to their fo'c's'le that Heavy discovered that his watches had been stolen.

When the mate released the watch, Mac and Nick stayed on deck for a few minutes to smoke a cigarette and cool off and watch the river roll by below them. Heavy left immediately at as close to a trot as he could manage.

"What's your hurry?" Nick asked. "It'll be hot as the hinges of hell in the fo'c's'le."

"I forgot something," Heavy said as he hurried away.

When Nick and Mac entered the fo'c's'le five minutes later, the fat man was on his knees, groping desperately under his bunk and cursing steadily.

"What's the matter?" Mac asked him. "You lose your collar button?"

Heavy bent as much as he could and tried to look under the bunk, but he was too bulky to get his head down far enough. He climbed to his feet and opened all three of the steel lockers that were provided for the watch and stared at their emptiness and then looked suspiciously at the seabags on Mac and Nick's bunks.

"They're gone," he said at last. "Some son of a bitch done stole my watches."

"What watches?" Nick asked. "You mean the watch you had fixed in New Orleans?"

Heavy was shaking with rage by now, and his little face was so suffused with blood that Nick was afraid he might collapse.

"The watches I bought to sell wherever we going," he said in a choked voice. "The watches I paid out five hundred bucks for. Some bastard done crept in here whilst we was workin' and stole 'em."

"The ones you picked up on the way to the commissioner?" Nick asked.

"That's them," Heavy said, turning hopefully to Nick. "Did you put them away somewhere?"

"Not me," Nick said. He looked at Mac, and Mac looked back, and Nick could see that Mac had the same suspicion that he had.

"Maybe Mac did something with them," Nick said quietly. "How about it, Mac?"

"Not me," Mac said. "Me, I didn't even know Heavy had any watches, did you, Nick?"

"No," Nick said. "I didn't figure that a man who had to send all that money to his poor old mother in jail in Bug Tussle, Texas, would have enough money to buy five hundred dollars' worth of watches."

"Don't hardly seem likely, do it?" Mac asked.

Heavy had listened to this exchange with growing trepidation, and now he broke in.

"Hey," he said, "I bought them watches last trip."

"You hid 'em real well," Mac said dryly. "And I guess you just plumb forgot to sell 'em?"

"I didn't get the chance," Heavy said sullenly.

"Let's see," Nick said. "You got a hundred bucks each from me and Mac and Stringbeans, and the watches cost five hundred bucks. Of course, you owe us the hundred in any case, but if you find the watches, I think I'll wait and see how much you get for them. I figure I got twenty per cent of the deal."

"Me too," Mac said. "Course, I ain't quite made up my mind if I want to take twenty per cent of the deal or take my share out of the fat man's hide."

Heavy argued long and vehemently, but Mac and Nick were adamant. Stringbeans, who looked in on his way to the crew's mess for coffee, agreed with them. The fat man was incoherent with rage by the time he lost the argument, and he stormed out of the fo'c's'le to demand that the captain stop the ship and search everyone on board.

Nick and Mac had gone to sleep by the time he got back, but he awakened them to complain about the captain's lack of understanding. He talked steadily until Nick reminded him that he was not supposed to have the watches, anyway.

"You better hope the captain wasn't paying much attention to you," Nick said. "If he remembers what you were talking about in the morning, you're in trouble."

"He didn't pay me no mind at all besides telling me to stow it," Heavy said. "He ain't gonna remember anything."

By the time the twelve-to-four ordinary called the watch, the *Andrew Crichton* was approaching the mouth of the Mississippi. Nick stood the wheel watch as the ship threaded its way through the southwest passage on its way out to the Gulf of Mexico.

When they had cleared the passage, the *Crichton* began to lose way as the pilot boat came alongside, and Nick's friend, the pilot, scrambled nimbly over the rail and down a rope ladder to the deck of the small craft. As the *Andrew Crichton* pulled away, he waved, and Nick waved back, although somehow he doubted that the pilot was waving at him. Dropping the pilot seemed, as always, a final good-bye to the land and the problems involved with it. He wondered briefly where the *Crichton* was bound, but he would not know for quite a while.

The mate kept the off watches working all day securing the ship for sea, so that by the time Nick took the wheel for the evening trick, he was tired and sleepy. It was clear now from the heading that the *Crichton* was steaming south along the West Coast of Florida. It was a good day, bright and warm, and the Gulf was flat and a glassy green under the sun.

Nick was steering from the flying bridge, checking the compass needle now and then to make sure he was keeping the course, but spending more time watching the sea or the deck gang at work forward.

The ship's carpenter was cementing the anchor on the forepeak, stopping up with cement the openings on deck through which the anchor chain dropped down into the chain locker so that seas breaking over the bow would not flood the chain locker. He finished and started aft just as the ship's bell rang twice, and Nick, as usual, had to do quick arithmetic to translate two bells into five o'clock. He speculated idly on why seamen could not tell time in the ordinary way aboard ship, but it did not seem important.

The captain and the chief mate were standing together by the forward rail of the bridge, talking in low voices, and Nick strained to hear what they were saying, hoping that the old man would drop a hint of the ship's destination. From the few words he caught, he learned they were going over the mate's work plans for the deck gang.

The navy gun crew had turned to on the guntubs, cleaning the 20-millimeters, and they knocked off when they heard two bells. It was a pleasant time of day; at sea, Nick sometimes felt a deep peace when the work day was over and the sea quiet, the ship plowing easily along with only the steady thump of the engine and an occasional voice from on deck to disturb the silence. It was like that now.

Mac was due to relieve the wheel at five twenty, and Nick, lulled into an agreeable torpor by the day and the flat hot sea, looked forward to a cup of coffee in the messroom. He had forgotten, for the moment, about the bosun and the problem of the tough steaks.

At ten minutes after five, the navy ensign in charge of the gun crew came up to the flying bridge and asked the captain for permission to give his crew gunnery practice.

The captain was an old man named Ole Haraldsen, and Nick knew, from the ship grapevine, that he had come out of retirement because of the war. He was a Norwegian, a tall, bony old man who had started his career in the days of sail, and Nick could see from the distaste on his face as he looked at the ensign that he did not like having a navy gun crew on board his ship. Nor did he like ensigns fresh out of a ninety-day naval training school.

The captain glared at the ensign for a long minute before he answered, and Nick forgot to watch his course as he saw the young man growing more and more nervous. The ensign was a plump, pink-faced youngster with round cheeks who looked like a sophomore on the campus of a small midwestern college.

Finally the old man sighed and said: "All right, mister. Regulations say I have to if there's no good reason why I shouldn't. But you will have to wait fifteen minutes."

"Thank you, sir," the ensign said, and saluted. The captain looked at him sourly, and Nick grinned. No one saluted in the merchant marine.

The ensign left to prepare the gun crew, and the first mate said, "Why did you want him to wait, sir?"

"Get everybody off the deck," the captain said. "I've seen these gun drills before. It's not safe on deck. Tell the bosun to detail the standby to see that the deck gang goes below before the firing starts."

The gun crew finished its makeready, and Nick glanced at the gunnery officer, who was standing at the rail on the flying bridge regarding his wristwatch intently, waiting for the fifteen minutes to pass.

Mac came up to relieve Nick as the mate left the bridge to give the bosun his instructions. Nick gave Mac the course, and Mac repeated it. Nick was on lookout for the next hour and twenty minutes, and he started to go down to the deck and forward to the bow, but Captain Haraldsen stopped him.

"Stay here," he said. "You'll be safer."

Nick grinned and said, "Aye, aye," and moved out to the wing of the bridge to watch the gunnery practice. The *Andrew Crichton* carried the normal armament of a merchant ship. There were a three-inch aft and a three-inch 24-millimeter forward; in guntubs on the wing of the bridge and fore and aft were 20-millimeter guns for antiaircraft fire.

For gunnery practice, an empty oil drum was dropped over the side for the crew on the aft big gun to shoot at. The big gun forward shot at whatever targets could be discovered on the surface of the sea ahead. Close inshore, as the ship was, the 20-millimeters could always find gulls to test their aim. The gulls were safe; Nick had never seen one so much as frightened by the firing.

Nick watched the crew on the starboard-wing guntub prepare for the drill. He had seen gunnery practice many times before in the two years he had been going to sea; some of the old gun crews were almost as sharp as fleet gunners, but this crew seemed as young and inexperienced as their officer.

On the rail of the guntub was a blinker light used in convoy for ship-to-ship communication during the day when ships could not break radio silence for fear submarines might intercept the signals and home in on it.

As the gun crew went about preparing for firing, no one paid any attention to the blinker, and Nick wondered if he should say anything. Navy gun crews were not partial to interference from the merchant seamen. Usually the first thing the gun crew did was to dismount the blinker to clear their field of fire.

The gun crew finished its makeready, and Nick glanced at the gunnery officer, who was standing at the rail of the flying bridge, still looking at his watch. Nick looked forward, and the decks were clear of merchant seamen; aft, only the gun crews in the tubs and on the big gun were in sight.

The sighter on the 20-millimeter in the guntub near Nick was tracking a gull as he waited; when the ensign gave the commence-firing order, he started shooting, the gun going *blam-blam-blam-blam* very fast, the shock of the explosions hurting Nick's ears so that he covered them with his hands.

All the other 20's were firing as well, and over the steady battering of their fire Nick could hear the regular *boom*s of the big guns fore and aft.

He looked toward the stern to see if the gun on the fantail was coming anywhere near the drum bobbing along far in the wake of the ship. He watched five shots, and decided that probably the safest place in that part of the Gulf of Mexico was on top of the drum.

Just as he turned back to watch the 20 on the wing of the bridge, the aimer started to track a gull flying low along a course that paralleled that of the ship. His bursts were behind the gull, and did not get any closer, and Nick thought later that at least his concentration must have been good, no matter how poor his marksmanship. In the next moment, he shot the blinker light off the rail of the guntub.

The 20's were loaded with explosive shells, and when the shell hit the blinker, it blew up and took out part of the rail and all the blinker and sprayed the flying bridge with hot shell fragments and debris. Nick dropped instinctively; when he got up from the deck, still not sure what had happened, the ensign was shouting "Cease fire!" at the top of his voice, which had gone high and squeaky. All the rest of the guns were firing as fast as their crews could serve them.

Nick looked around the bridge quickly, expecting to see dead or wounded men on the deck, but no one was down. The ensign had moved to the intercom, trying to get his cease-fire message across to the gun stations; and slowly, one at a time, the guns quit firing. The last gun to fire a round was the big gun on the fantail; the oil drum was barely visible far astern, and the splash of the shell was easily a quarter of a mile short.

Nick's ears were ringing in the silence following the last futile shot; for a moment he thought he had been deafened. Then he saw Captain Haraldsen come out from behind the ventilator where he had taken refuge, and walk slowly across to the guntub to survey the damage.

One member of the gun crew had a small cut on his forehead, and the captain inspected the scratch thoughtfully. The ensign was leaning on the rail, looking dazed and a little sick; the gunners looked puzzled. There was still no sound, and Nick rapped himself smartly on the side of the head with the butt of his hand, trying to clear his ears.

The captain walked slowly back to the ensign, and Nick followed him, hoping he had not lost his hearing for good. He wanted to hear what the old man would say to the ensign. He expected an explosion, but the captain, when he finally spoke, sounded more hurt than angry. Nick marveled at his self-control.

When the captain came to within an arm's length of the ensign, he stopped and looked at him mournfully for a while. Then he said: "Mr. Lockridge, there will be no more crap like that aboard my vessel unless we are under direct attack by at least two submarines and several squadrons of airplanes. If that should happen, I will give you my permission to commence firing as soon as I have taken off the entire crew. I would like to have time to abandon ship before you blow us out of the water."

Mr. Lockridge looked at the captain blankly for a moment, then said, "Wait a moment, sir," and fished rubber plugs out of his ears.

"I'm sorry, sir," he said. "I didn't hear you."

"Don't shoot those God-damn guns anymore!" the captain roared, and Nick put his hands over his ears again. The gun practice had been no louder.

The ensign put his earplugs back in and nodded sadly and gave the gun crews the order to secure. Nick waited a while to see if the captain would have anything else to say to him, but the old man had lapsed into a brooding silence, and Nick went below to eat. By the time he reached the crew's mess, most of the men off watch were eating, and he was forced to take a seat across the table from the bosun. He thought for a moment about taking Heavy's suggestion and going to his fo'c's'le for his foul-weather gear, but he decided instead he would hope for a minimum of sibilants in the bosun's conversation.

Nick would have preferred to avoid the bosun in any case. The bosun was busily gumming a pork chop when Nick sat down, and the old man did not speak for some time, but Nick's faint hope that he had forgotten the case of the unchewable steak was shortlived.

Nick had ordered and was waiting for the messboy to bring his plate when the bosun looked up from the pork chop and fixed him with a bleary stare. The old man put down his chop and waved a greasy finger at Nick.

"Mr. Deck Delegate," he said, "they're still feeding out of two potsh, jush like I told you. Thish is the skinniest pork chop I ever laid my teeth into."

"Laid gums onto," Nick murmured.

"Whatsh that?" Boats said.

"Nothing," Nick told him.

The bosun held up the pork chop for Nick to see. It did look fairly anemic.

"I'll go up to the saloon mess as soon as I finish eating," Nick told the bosun. The messboy brought him his own pork chops and string beans and mashed potatoes, and he ate as slowly as he could, hoping forlornly that the bosun would grow tired of waiting and go away.

He did not. He stumped away to his fo'c's'le, but he soon returned with a dirty and dog-eared copy of the union contract, and read the section on food aloud for Nick's benefit.

Nick knew the contract from his previous experience as

a deck delegate. It said clearly that officers and crew were to be fed food of the same quantity and quality, even to the thickness and grade of the meat.

The rest of the crew was listening to the bosun by now, and a fireman on Stringbeans' watch said, "It's the dirty capitalists, that's who it is." Nick had noticed him at breakfast; he was another old-timer like the bosun, and almost as unprepossessing, as well as being even dirtier.

Now he pulled a greasy micrometer caliper out of his overalls and offered it to Nick.

"Here," he said. "Go measure the officers' pork chops."

"I'm the deck delegate," Nick protested. "You tell the engine-room delegate to go measure the pork chops. I don't even know how to read one of those things."

"*I'm* the engine-room delegate," the fireman said. "I'm Joey the Shovel."

"Why don't you go up, then?" Nick said. "I'm not through eating."

"You both got to go together," the bosun said. "It makes it more official."

"I'll measure the pork chops in here while you finish," Joey told Nick.

Nick finished his dinner reluctantly while Joey the Shovel measured pork chops. Joey took thickness measurements on four pork chops he selected at random in the messroom, then calculated an average thickness. The seamen whose pork chops he measured did not seem particularly charmed by the idea, but they did not protest; and when Joey had finished, he wiped off his micrometer carefully and announced the results.

"Thickest one was 1.38 centimeters," he said portentously. "Thinnest one was 1.26, and I figure the average of the four of them was 1.31. Now, I ain't any pork-chop expert, but I bet the bosun is right and they got thicker ones than that topside."

Nick was nibbling slowly at his dessert by then, trying to think of something to postpone the visit to the saloon mess. Joey the Shovel, who seemed to enjoy the floor, was explaining that he was called Joey the Shovel because he had started firing in the engine room when firemen had to shovel coal instead of regulating the flow of oil. He pointed out that even then the capitalist bosses were growing fat by feeding seamen thin pork chops; then he turned to Nick.

"We don't get up there pretty soon, they gonna eat up all the evidence," he said. "Come on, Deck. You can finish your ice cream when we get back."

"If we get back," Nick said as he rose to his feet. He followed the fireman out of the mess room unhappily, and with a sense of doom.

7

Most of the officers had finished eating when Nick and Joey the Shovel walked into the saloon mess. Only Captain Haraldsen and Ensign Stockbridge still had food on their plates. The captain still looked angry, and the ensign's head was down as he ate quickly. The old man must have been chewing him out some more, Nick thought.

The rest of the officers were drinking coffee and talking quietly, but they stopped when Nick and Joey the Shovel came in. Joey looked around for the chief engineer, but Nick decided he had left. Joey turned to Nick and said, "You tell the old man."

"You have the measurements," Nick said. "You tell him."

Captain Haraldsen had looked up from his meal and was

watching them now, and Nick could tell by the flush spreading over his craggy face that he was about to explode. Nick tried to think of a diplomatic way to broach the subject of the relative thickness of the meats in the saloon and crew's mess, but nothing occurred to him offhand.

"Go on," Joey the Shovel said impatiently. "We ain't got all night. I got to get my sleep."

"What the hell is this?" Captain Haraldsen asked. He had just begun to eat, and he had two pork chops on his plate. Nick looked at them closely to see if they seemed any thicker than the pork chops served in the crew's mess, but they looked about the same.

I might as well get it over with, he thought, and plunged in.

"Sir, I want to measure your pork chops. That is, Joey wants to measure your pork chops," he said rapidly.

The captain suddenly looked very tired and very old, and Nick felt a quick spasm of sympathy for him.

Captain Haraldsen turned painfully toward his first mate and looked at him questioningly.

"Mr. Mate," he said, "it has been a long time. I suppose I am not as young as I used to be. I thought I heard this man say he wanted to measure my pork chops, but I must have been wrong. He didn't say that, did he?"

"I didn't hear him," the first said diplomatically.

The captain turned back to Nick and said, patiently, "What did you say, sailor?"

Nick was trying desperately to think of another way to phrase his request when Joey the Shovel broke in.

"We want to measure your pork chops," he said. "You feeding out of two pots on this, Captain. And that's against the union contract. Deck and black gang."

The captain got up slowly and walked away down the saloon mess a few feet. There he stood for a full minute with his back to Nick and Joey the Shovel. As soon as he turned his back, Joey snatched a pork chop from his plate and clapped the calipers on it and said to Nick: "I told you so. Put this down, Deck. It's one point four three."

Nick wrote the figures down in a small notebook. It was so quiet that the scratching sound of the pencil on paper seemed loud. The officers were watching Joey the Shovel in awful fascination, as if they could not believe what they were seeing. Nick finished his notation, and Joey picked up the other pork chop on the captain's plate and began to measure it just as the captain turned around.

"One point two eight," said Joey the Shovel, disappointed.

"We got to get two more to get a average." He looked across the table at the ensign's plate. Everyone else had finished eating, and the ensign had the only full plate on the table other than the captain's. The ensign saw Joey looking at his pork chops, and leaned over his plate with his elbows spread to protect the chops.

"Put my pork chop down," the captain said slowly. Joey put the captain's pork chop back on the captain's plate and walked around the table toward the ensign. Every head in the saloon mess turned to follow him.

Captain Haraldsen came back to his chair and looked down at the pork chops and then looked at Joey. Joey was doing his best to get by the ensign's guard to reach a pork chop, and Nick had to admire the defense the ensign was putting up. He blocked each of Joey's moves while everyone watched intently and silently, including the captain.

When Nick finally tore his eyes from the duel between Joey and Mr. Lockridge to look at the captain, Haraldsen's face was beginning to flush, and Nick, remembering the explosion on the bridge, started to edge toward the door. Joey was still making quick grabs at the ensign's pork chops, and

Lockridge was blocking with his arms and elbows while everyone watched.

Nick looked back at the captain and was just opening his mouth to say something when an anguished scream broke the silence.

Joey the Shovel had finally penetrated the ensign's defense and laid a hand on one of the pork chops, and the ensign, in a belated attempt to save it, had stabbed with his fork and got Joey in the back of the hand.

The ensign jumped to his feet, and Joey looked down at his hand with the fork embedded in it. So did Nick and the captain and everyone else. The ensign backed away two steps, his face white, and Joey pulled the fork out of his hand and picked up the pork chop and measured it.

"One point three eight," he said, and Nick made the notation in his notebook automatically.

Joey's hand was bleeding on the tablecloth, but he paid no attention to it. He picked up the ensign's second pork chop and measured that one. "One point four four."

Nick wrote it down. He had quit thinking when Joey made his sortie against the ensign; he felt as if he were somewhere outside the saloon mess, watching this scene as a spectator, not a part of it.

The purser was the first officer to move. He came over to Joey the Shovel and said, "I better attend to that wound, my good man." The purser doubled as a pharmacist's mate, as did all pursers on merchant ships. Now he took Joey's hand and looked at it carefully and said, judiciously, "Four simple puncture wounds, complicated by gravy."

Joey the Shovel pulled his hand away from the purser and sucked at the back of it, then licked his fingers where he had picked up the pork chops.

"Different gravy," he said. "Put that down, Deck Delegate."

Nick wrote down "different gravy" in his notebook, numbly. "Maybe it's the blood," he said. "That might change the taste." He added "possibly blood" to his notes.

The captain, in a strangled voice, said, "Purser, attend to that man."

The purser reached for Joey's hand again, but Joey held it away from him.

"Captain," said Joey very formally, "I ain't figured out the average yet, but it appears to me that my measurements prove that the pork chops in the saloon mess are thicker than the pork chops served in the crew's mess. I and the deck delegate here, we're going to make a official protest, and if it ain't fixed, we'll take it up with the commissioner when we sign off this ship."

"Yes," the captain said tightly, "and I'm logging you and the deck delegate for insubordination. And we'll take that up with the commissioner, too."

"I got witnesses," Joey said. "Ever'body in here seen me measure them pork chops. And the deck wrote down the figures."

"If you don't want to spend the rest of this trip in the chain locker," the captain said ominously, "you'd better get out of here."

"Threatening a union official in the performance of his duties," Joey said to Nick. "Write that down, too."

"I must attend to that hand," said the purser officiously, but Joey paid no attention to him.

"Get out!" the captain yelled, and started around the table toward Joey and Nick.

Nick was out of the door in two long, quick steps, but Joey the Shovel stood his ground for another second.

"And I got stabbed by a naval officer on a merchant ship," Joey said to the captain. "I ain't read the union rules on that, but they must be something on it. Put it down, Deck."

Nick put it down as he trotted along the companionway on his way down to the crew's messroom, where the bosun and the rest of the deck and black-room gangs were waiting for them. Joey went in ahead of Nick, as if he were leading a parade.

8

Captain Haraldsen logged Nick
and Joey the Shovel ten days' pay, but Nick did not worry
about it. He knew that no maritime commissioner would back
up a log against union delegates on union business, and, no
matter how unorthodox Joey's approach had been, he was still
within his rights in insisting upon equal quality and quantity
of food for officers and crew. Joey the Shovel wanted to go
back the next night and measure the meat again, but Nick persuaded him that it would be easier to do the measuring in the
galley before the meat went up to the saloon mess.

They went in while the chief cook was carving steaks,
and watched him; then Joey measured the steaks and found
that they were all about the same thickness.

"How do I know you ain't going to cut off some more steaks for the saloon mess as soon as my back is turned?" Joey asked the chief cook.

"Stay and watch as long as you want to, mon," the cook said indifferently. "I be a good union mon, too. I don't feed from no two pots, mon."

Joey stayed and watched, but Nick went back into the messroom and ate, sure that the cook was right. He had to admit to himself that the steaks on this night seemed tenderer and thicker than they had the night before.

By now the *Andrew Crichton* was two days at sea and nearing the tip of Florida, and the crew waited anxiously to find which way the ship would turn. Nick and most of the rest of the crew wanted the ship to stay in the Caribbean, where the air and the water were warm and the submarines not so numerous as they were in the Atlantic. But when the new course was given, the *Crichton* was on a northerly heading, rounding the tip of Florida for the long trip up the Atlantic Coast toward New York.

"We'll probably pick up a convoy outside of New York and head across the North Atlantic for Europe or the Mediterranean," Mac said. "We'll be out in the middle of the North Atlantic in late September, cold as a well digger's ass in Alaska."

"We probably headed for Murmansk," Heavy said bitterly. "And I could of sold them watches for a fortune in Murmansk, from what I been told. Now I got to go and get my ass shot off for nothing."

He and Nick and Mac had just come off watch, and were sitting on the coaming of the Number One hatch, near the bow of the ship. To port, between the *Andrew Crichton* and the Florida mainland, they could see a red glow on the horizon. The coastal cities of Florida were blacked out so that their lights would not silhouette merchant ships for the submarines infesting the Atlantic. The glow, he guessed, was a tanker burning after a torpedo attack. He had seen tankers every night on previous trips along the Atlantic Coast.

"We may not make it to the North Atlantic," Nick said.

"We'll probably pick up a convoy," Mac insisted. "If we get that far."

He looked at the red glow on the edge of the sea.

"I figure it's about six to five," he said. "Against."

"Against Murmansk?" Nick asked.

"Against making the convoy rendezvous," Mac said.

"Anyway, we're not headed for Murmansk," Nick told him.

"How you know?" Heavy asked. "The old man show you the order?"

"No," Nick replied. "But they didn't insulate the fo'c's'les before we left port. They always do that if you're on your way to Murmansk." "They'll probably do it in New York," Heavy said gloomily. "They know they got us by the balls then. We already signed on. Be just my luck. Freeze to death just because you guys start a fight. Just because Nick got to knock up a B girl."

"It was you sat on her brother and probably squatted him to death," Nick said. "I didn't kill him."

"You don't know he's dead," Heavy said. "And it's all your fault. You keep on doing the way you do with the ladies, and we ain't gonna have a safe port in the world to put into."

He was silent for a while, his grotesque body slumped uncomfortably on the edge of the hatch.

"Even if we don't go to Murmansk, I ain't gonna get any sleep for a couple weeks," he said sadly. "What with the bunks and the watches, I'm gonna be worrying or wobbling from now until we make port somewhere."

"Part of them watches was ours," Mac said. "Don't forget it."

"You ain't got my sleeping problem," Heavy said.

Nick grinned, thinking of Heavy's difficulties in foul weather. The bunks in a Liberty ship were built athwartships so that when the ship rolled in a heavy sea, you slept standing on your head one moment and on your feet the next. Nick had grown used to the movement, and could sleep through it comfortably, but he knew Heavy could not. If he slept on his back, his belly slid up under his chin when the ship rolled to port, and sagged back down between his legs when it rolled to starboard.

It was no help for him to sleep on his belly. If he tried that, he rocked back and forth over his paunch like a teeter-totter on a vast soft pillow. He could not sleep on his side because his stomach dangled over the edge of the bunk and swung back and forth like a pendulum.

Nick looked sympathetically at Heavy now. The fat man was perched on the edge of the hatch, with his legs spread and his belly hanging down between them, looking as woe-begone and petulant as a small child who had just dropped an ice-cream cone.

Stringbeans was coming forward along the deck, and Heavy was watching him. Stringbeans, as usual, walked with a free and easy gait. He was doing a little shuffle step now and then, jabbing at the air with his right hand.

"Man, you should of seen me oiling," he said happily when he reached them. "You ain't never seen such a fancy oiler. I'm hitting the bearings left and right like this, and squirting the oil four feet and making it right where I want it. The first assistant like to died just watching."

He skipped about, pantomiming squirting oil over his shoulder and behind his back and between his legs, and Heavy shook his head in disgust.

"You a load," he said. "You're too much, Stringbeans. Any man gets his kicks oiling on a Liberty."

"They's worst things," Stringbeans said. He sat down and looked at the red aura dying out astern of the *Andrew Crichton.* "They is lots of worst things," he said softly.

It was too dark by now to light a cigarette. The glow had faded, but Nick could still see a red track over the surface of the water, and the four men were quiet for a few minutes. Nick wondered why anyone would ship out on a tanker.

The light blinked out quickly, and Stringbeans sighed. "Poor bastards," he said. "She's down. Ain't even no oil burning on the water no more. Poor bastards."

"Worry about us, not them," Mac said, his face thin with the wide-mouth grim. "You better hope he went the other way after he got that tanker."

"He got to be running for cover," Stringbeans said. "Coast guard all around here, man. He got to lie quiet on the bottom for a long time, and hope they don't smell him out."

The navy gun crew had been at general quarters, standing by their guns. They usually secured at sundown, but with the tanker burning in the wake, the ensign had kept them on station. He must be as nervous as I am, Nick thought. That's pretty nervous.

It was full dark by now, and Nick wanted a cigarette badly.

"You want to play some gin?" he asked Heavy.

"Okay," the fat man said. "But you got to put the cards down right. You always put them down sideways so I can't read them."

Nick was depressed as they walked back down the deck toward the midship house. He could not shake the thought of the men dying on the burning tanker; he had been torpedoed twice, but once the ship had been carrying general cargo. The other time it was carrying timber, and neither time had it caught fire. He tried to imagine the inferno of a burning tanker, but it was impossible.

They went through the blackout screens and into the crew's mess, and Heavy broke out his cards. An ordinary from another watch sat down by Heavy to watch, but Heavy chased him away.

"Don't sit there and make signs to Nick," he said irritably. "Go sit down by him if you got to watch the game. Ain't you on lookout or something?"

"I'm on standby," the ordinary said with an injured air. He was a skinny, pimply boy, and Nick did not know him. There was no reason for Heavy to think that he would help Nick in the game, but, since his watches had been stolen, Heavy was an even more suspicious man than usual.

They played two hands, and Nick was on the board twice and Heavy had not scratched yet. He was getting more and more unhappy, and Nick figured that the game would last about a half hour before Heavy ripped the deck to bits, unless he won a few hands.

Mac and Stringbeans and Johnny, a short, dark Italian deckhand who was an acting AB on the eight-to-twelve watch, were playing poker with the navy coxswain. The coxswain was a small, wiry red-haired man named, naturally, Red. Nick was anxious for Heavy to give up so that he could get in the poker game, but Heavy won two hands in quick succession, and the poker game broke up when Johnny had to go on watch and Red left to sack out.

Heavy was dealing the next hand, and Mac and String-beans were trying to decide whether to wait for the ordinary from the next watch to come in for a three-handed game of poker or whether to play gin when the first assistant engineer came in. The mess hall was not officers' country; officers did not come into the crew's mess unless it was to find someone for a job, so Nick thought at first that the engineer had come in looking for Stringbeans to stand a watch.

But he sat down next to Heavy, and paid no attention to Stringbeans. He had a half-full water tumbler in his hand, and he watched silently while Heavy dealt the hand.

"You looking for me, First?" Stringbeans asked after a while.

"Nope," said the engineer, and drank from his water tumbler. "I ain't looking for nobody. I like it better in the crew's mess. Sailed below all my life, and never sailed higher than oiler until the God-damn war started. Now they got me sailing first assistant."

He sipped at his water glass again.

"Good money, ain't it?" Stringbeans asked noncommitally.

The first assistant engineer looked at Stringbeans for a long moment before answering. He was a short, wide, fat man but not fat the way Heavy was fat. Heavy was soft fat; the engineer was hard fat. Looking at him curiously, Nick thought that his was strong, muscular fat, his arms thick and stuffed with sinew, the way Tony Galento had been when he could fight. The first assistant was a little bleary-eyed, and it took him a long time to understand what Stringbeans had asked him. When it penetrated, he shook his head and drank again before he answered.

"Money's all right," he said then. "It's just I don't like the people I got to associate with topside. Like the chief engineer on this ship. He's a raunchy old bastard."

The first assistant was the equivalent, in the engine room, of the first mate on deck. He ran the black gang under the overall supervision of the chief engineer, just as the first mate ran the deck gang under the eye of the captain. Stringbeans, as an oiler, ranked the same as Mac or Nick, who were able-bodied seamen. Heavy, an ordinary seaman on deck, would have been a wiper in the engine room.

The first assistant took another sip from his water glass, and belched heartily. Nick, sitting across from him, had thought he was drinking water, but the fumes from the belch were pure grain alcohol.

He was drinking the alcohol straight. Stringbeans told Nick later that the first stole it from the supply on hand for the ship's refrigeration system.

"I been watching you," the first said to Stringbeans solemnly. "Dancing around down there, squirting oil behind your back and between your legs. You some kind of damn fairy or something?" Nick, now that he realized what the engineer was drinking, could see that he was very drunk. Although he did not slur his speech, he talked very slowly and with the exaggerated care some drunks use at their drunkest.

"He's a bogalee," Heavy said. "That's worse."

The first turned his head slowly on his short, thick neck and studied Heavy for a long time, then sipped his grain alcohol.

"Ain't you the damnedest-looking sailor I ever seen?" he said at last. He shook his head in disbelief. "If I could get you down below, I'd melt enough tallow off you to waterproof a set of sail for a three-master. What in hell do you *do*?"

"I'm an ordinary seaman," Heavy said. He was trying to concentrate on his gin-rummy game, but the first assistant had distracted him, and when he discarded a king, Nick picked it up, and grinned.

"That was a stupid play," the first assistant observed owlishly. "Wasn't that a stupid play, Mr. Fancy Oiler?" He looked at Stringbeans.

"I quit," Heavy said angrily. "It ain't enough I got to have some cracker-ass ordinary stand behind me and tell my cards. Now I got to have a fat-ass first assistant engineer come in the crew's mess where he don't even belong and sit next to me and breathe alcohol on me until I can't read the cards for my eyes watering, and beyond that, he's got to bad-mouth me."

He tried to get up quickly, but it was impossible at the mess table. The chairs were bolted to the deck; they were swivel chairs, and the space allowed between the back of the chair and the edge of the table was calculated for men of ordinary girth, not for Heavy.

To sit at the table, he had to turn a chair sideways, sit down in it, then swing it gradually around until he was facing the table, moving slowly so that he would not hurt himself. Nick had once suggested that he butter his belly first, but Heavy had not taken kindly to that idea. By the time he was facing forward, the edge of the table made a big dent in his stomach. Sometimes, after a particularly gargantuan meal, it would take him fifteen or twenty minutes to free himself from his chair.

Now he was easing his chair around gently, moving slowly and carefully so that he would not bruise his stomach. The first assistant stood up and put his glass on the mess table.

"Lemme help," he said with mock solicitude. He grabbed the back of Heavy's chair and gave it a powerful spin. Heavy went all the way around once, and then stuck facing the table again.

"Don't help me no more," Heavy said bitterly, craning to look at the first, who was still standing behind his chair. "You liked to of ruined my stomach. I don't need no more help like that."

Nick looked at the engineer, and started to get up to help Heavy, but the first, who seemed to be growing drunker by the moment, lost interest in Heavy, and sat down. He took another drink of grain alcohol and focused his eyes, with difficulty, on Stringbeans. Nick could see that he was trying to work out what he wanted to say. Heavy started easing his way around in the seat again, and the first assistant ignored him.

"How come you oil like that?" the first asked.

"Makes it more fun," Stringbeans said. "Ain't every oiler you ever seen who can hit the spot he's aiming at the way I can, First. Especially not backwards between his legs."

Heavy had worked himself free again by now, and was resting from his exertions. He was watching the first assistant balefully, and breathing heavily.

"God-damn kook," he muttered.

"Shut up," the first said. He got up and gave Heavy another twirl, and the fat man was stuck again. "I wasn't talking to you, fatso," the first said.

"Besides, I got a very strong feeling for them bearings," Stringbeans went on. "Hurts me if any of 'em gets overheated."

"You talk about them like they was alive," the first said. "They ain't."

"To me they is," Stringbeans said. "Sometimes I think I purely care more for a smooth-running bearing than I do for a fine lady. Some fine ladies, that is."

Red, the navy coxswain, had returned to the messroom, and was listening with interest. He had bright blue eyes, a thick sprinkling of freckles, and a serious outlook on life. He had been in the navy for more than twenty years, and Nick liked him.

"How come it always got to happen to me?" he asked no one in particular, shaking his head. "Last trip, I shipped with a guy fell in love with a 20-millimeter gun. Had to haul him off the ship kicking and screaming because the gunnery officer wouldn't let him dismantle it and take it to bed with him. Called the gun Josephine, and he used to sit in the gun tub and talk to her even when he wasn't on duty."

"He must have been a real nut," Nick said.

"No worse than this here oiler," the first said. "There

ain't much to choose between a main bearing and a 20-milli-
meter, seems to me. Don't seem to me like a man's gonna get
much satisfaction from either one."

"This guy was pretty happy," Red said. "Josephine used
to talk back to him."

"What did she say?" Mac said.

"Told him once it made her throat sore during gunnery
practice," Red said. "That's why they had to take him off the
ship. He wouldn't pull her trigger one time in the Mediterranean when we were under air attack."

"I ain't never talked to no main bearings," Stringbeans
said indignantly. "And ain't no main bearing ever said nothing to me, either."

"That do make a difference," Heavy said. He had finally
extricated himself from his chair, and was edging toward the
door. "Anything I can't stand, it's a woman who always got
to talk, talk, talk."

"Fat as you are, you ought to be glad to get any kind,"
the first assistant said. "How you manage with that great big
belly on you, anyway?"

"You ain't exactly a candidate for thin man in the cir-
cus," Heavy told him. He was close to the door and he moved
a little closer. "And you're a hell of a lot uglier than me, too.
You wouldn't be a bargain for a main bearing or a 20-
millimeter gun."

"But I got more money," the first said. He had nearly
finished the grain alcohol, and he stood up, prompting Heavy
to skip quickly out the door. The first laughed at him, and
tossed off the rest of his drink.

"Don't go away," he said to Stringbeans, "I'm going to
bring back a whole bottle of this here. I know you ain't gonna
be able to drink it the way I do, but you can get the messboy
to break out some fruit juice. It ain't bad that way."

He walked out steadily, without staggering.

"Does he drink like that on watch?" Nick asked Stringbeans.

"Not so's you can tell," Stringbeans said. "Leastways, he ain't too bad to stand watch with. Seems like a pretty good head most of the time."

"Trouble," Red said. The little coxswain shook his head sorrowfully. "He's gonna be trouble. You watch and see."

"Ain't much else I can do," Stringbeans said philosophically. "Ain't no place to get off out here."

The first assistant did not come back with the grain alcohol, and Nick felt a faint disappointment. He had looked forward to a drink, and the straight grapefruit juice the messboy had brought was not a satisfactory substitute. He won twenty dollars playing poker with Mac, Stringbeans, and Red before he and Mac retired to their fo'c's'le to get some sleep before the morning watch.

Heavy was lying in his bunk reading when they came in, scratching his feet against each other.

"Why the hell don't you get rid of that athlete's foot?" Mac asked him irritably. "You gonna wind up giving it to me and Nick."

"I don't never let it get out of control," Heavy said contentedly. "I like to keep it just a little itchy but not real hurty. It feels good scratching it that way. Ain't many things you can do at sea feels as good as scratching a little bitty case of athlete's foot."

"Jesus," Mac said as he and Nick prepared to go to bed. "One buddy's in love with the main bearings and another gets his jollies scratching between his toes. Lucky me and you is okay, Nick."

"Takes time," Nick said, and grinned. "By the time we've been shipping for a few more years, you can't tell what we'll be in love with."

"You figure the first could of stole my watches?" Heavy asked. "Seemed like a shifty type to me."

"I doubt it," Nick said. He rolled over on his side with his back to Heavy, and tried to lose himself in a book. The trip was starting as usual. Situation normal, he thought, and grinned to himself. All fucked up.

9

Going east up the Atlantic Coast, the *Andrew Crichton* ran into heavy weather off Cape Hatteras. Nick welcomed it; foul weather never disturbed him, and it was less likely that they would have trouble from submarines as long as the clouded nights were black and the seas heavy. But there was one defect in the *Andrew Crichton* that grew steadily worse as the weather held bad.

It began to blow just before Nick went off watch in the evening of their fourth day at sea, and Heavy cursed steadily for the next four hours, trying to hold his belly still. By the time the twelve-to-four watch went on duty, Nick thought the *Liberty* must be dipping her stack on some of her rolls. She would heel far over, lie on her side for what seemed like minutes, shudder slightly, then come back slowly and heel over just as far the other way, to the accompaniment of the crash of pots and pans falling in the galley.

Nick expected the captain to change course during the twelve-to-four so that the *Andrew Crichton* would be meeting the big seas head on. She was taking cruel punishment from the beam seas, but apparently Captain Haraldsen wanted to hold course as long as possible before standing out to sea. Must be a close-convoy rendezvous, Nick thought. He was in the messroom trying to juggle a half cup of coffee and drink it in the rare moments when the ship was still.

Just before the ordinary seaman on the twelve-to-four came to call Nick and the rest of his watch, the ship's motion changed, and Nick could tell that the new course was quartering into the seas. Now the Liberty would lift by the bow, roll, kick her stern into the air until Nick could feel the vibration when the screw spun out of the water, then roll the other way and lift again. No fancy oiling for Stringbeans on this watch, Nick thought.

After the ordinary told him it was ten minutes until time to relieve the watch, Nick made his way to the head before taking the wheel. Four navy boots were hanging over the johns, as green as the Gulf seas, and, Nick judged by their dry heaves, as empty as gourds. We would be in a hell of a mess if we were attacked by Indians in canoes, Nick thought, let alone by a submarine. No one to man the guns.

He struggled into his foul-weather gear and went back to the crew's mess for a quick cup of coffee. The chief cook had turned-to most of the mess gang so that they could clean up the pots and pans and food scattered across the galley deck and the messroom. He had coffee working in the big coffee machine, and Nick poured himself another half cup and gulped it down scalding hot between wallows of the ship.

Heavy joined him and bitched at the chief cook because

he wouldn't bring out the night lunch that was usually on the table for the watch coming off duty. Most of the cold cuts and bread were on the deck, and Heavy poured himself a cup of coffee. Nick laughed when the fat man spilled most of it over himself trying to drink at the peak of a roll, and Heavy cursed him automatically.

"Tough weather for you," Nick said. He felt sorry for the fat man. Nick usually had an unreasonable sense of well-being in stormy weather, but Heavy suffered noisily.

Nick finished his coffee and went up to the bridge, pulling himself along by the handrails when the ship heeled far over. He took the course from the AB on the wheel; the first mate and the captain were both in the wheelhouse, staring out the square ports at the weather. I don't know what the hell they can see, Nick thought. It's black as a witch's heart out there.

The only light in the wheelhouse was the shaded light on the binnacle, showing the face of the compass. Nick braced himself against the wheel and worked at trying to keep the compass needle on the heading. It swung wildly back and forth, and Nick tried to keep the swings roughly the same on both sides of the heading. He had to put on two full turns of right wheel against the push of the quartering sea, and he remembered what the Mississippi River pilot had said. She really was difficult in a quartering sea.

"You think maybe we should bring her head on into the seas?" the mate asked the captain, and Haraldsen shook his head.

"I never missed a convoy rendezvous yet," the tall old man said stubbornly. "I ain't about to now, mister. Keep her steady as she goes."

"Steady as she goes," the mate said to Nick, who repeated the command. He put on another half-turn of right wheel because the *Andrew Crichton* was beginning to fall off.

It took a long time for the ship to answer. When the bow finally swung slowly back, Nick had to put on another half-turn of wheel just to hold her. And in a few minutes, she began to slip off the heading again. Nick brought the wheel over to check her, and was shocked to find it at hard right, all the way over against the stops.

He realized then what had been happening as the ship fought the quartering sea. On some Liberties, if you had to hold a couple of turns of wheel for a long time, right or left, the hydraulic fluid in the steering cylinder leaked from one side of the cylinder to the other.

The hydraulic system in the binnacle shaft transmitted the turn of the wheel to the steering engines in the engine room, and the engines actually turned the rudder. The longer you had to hold right or left wheel, the more fluid leaked around the piston, and the less wheel you had left. Eventually you could put the wheel hard right, as Nick was doing now, and the steering engine would hold the rudder for a dead-ahead course. You had no wheel left.

That was what had happened, and Nick knew that something had to be done quickly. He called the mate and told him he had no wheel left. The mate came over, watched the compass needle swinging farther and farther off the course, and asked, "How much wheel you got on her now?"

"All there is," Nick said.

"God damn," the mate said dispassionately, and called to Captain Haraldsen.

The captain stared at the compass for a while, his craggy old face worried; then he asked Nick, "How much wheel you got on her, sailor?"

Nick tried to put on more right wheel, but the helm was jammed hard against the stops.

"It's up against the stops now," he said. "Nothing left, sir."

The *Andrew Crichton* had swung into the trough of the sea by now, and she was rolling wildly. The mate and the captain were hanging on the binnacle, fighting to keep their feet, and Nick was holding himself up by bracing himself against the wheel. In the saloon mess on the deck below, he could hear the clatter of pots and pans and, faintly, the cursing of the saloon messboy.

"Don't just stand there, mister," the captain yelled at the mate. "Open up the binnacle and equalize the cylinder."

"Aye, aye," the mate said. He got down on his knees in front of the compass and opened the binnacle so he could get at the cylinder. He was crouched directly in front of Nick, on the other side of the binnacle, and Nick could not see what he was doing.

"Put her amidships lively when I give you the word," he said to Nick, and Nick said, "Aye, aye, sir." Captain Haraldsen was hanging on the binnacle, watching the mate. Nick felt the wheel go slack, and at the same time the mate yelled, "Midship!" Nick spun the wheel amidship.

He had expected to feel some life in the wheel, but it was as loose as the roulette wheel in a carnival game. He started to say something to the mate, but the captain said, "God Almighty!" and dropped out of sight.

Startled, Nick did not know where he had gone until the ship rolled hard to starboard, and Nick saw the captain, on his back, sailing majestically from port to starboard across the deck at the front of the wheelhouse, his feet in the air. Nick was surprised that he was sliding instead of rolling over the steel plating.

Captain Haraldsen fetched up stern first against the door leading out onto the deck, and hung while the Liberty shuddered and began to recover; as she heeled over to port, he slowly gathered headway on his return journey across the wheelhouse, and Nick watched him with fascination.

The mate's head suddenly popped up in front of Nick, and he said, "The pet cock came out, and the hydraulic oil is leaking out on the deck." He started to say something else, but the ship rolled heavily and he kicked twice, clutching desperately at the binnacle, reminding Nick fleetingly of a Russian dancer. Then he disappeared, and the next time Nick saw him, he had joined the captain. The two of them were skidding rapidly over the oil-wet deck to the starboard bulkhead.

They made swimming motions while the *Crichton* shuddered, then started to roll back, and they began to move again, side by side. Captain Haraldsen was still on his back; the mate had struggled to his hands and knees, balancing precariously. Both of them were trying to turn themselves so they would come into the port bulkhead stern to instead of headfirst.

As they swooped past the binnacle, the mate hollered, "Call the engine room—" but before he could say more, he banged butt foremost into the wall. The captain, looking like a large and clumsy insect that had been turned on its back, hit broadside. With no rudder, the *Crichton* was wallowing sickeningly, lying over on her beam-ends with each roll.

The mate started his turn at once, as he left the wall to cross the wheelhouse, and so did the captain. Nick could see that they were developing a certain skill at navigating on the oil-slick deck. As they came by him on this lap, gathering speed and turning slowly, the mate continued, "—and get the first assistant up here!" he yelled just before he hit the far bulkhead.

Nick was not anxious to give up his grip on the wheel to cross the bucking wheelhouse to the engine-room speaking tube. The deck was wet and slippery with the oil, and he had all he could do to keep his feet, even though he was braced by the wheel.

The captain had managed to flip over on his belly, and he came by traveling sideways, facing Nick. He yelled, "*Call the engine room, damn it!*" just before he hit again, so Nick decided he had better try.

"Aye, aye, sir!" he called, and poised himself.

He waited until the Liberty shuddered on her side between rolls. Then Nick set out on a crabbed course, as if he were tacking into the wind, first up the slope, then down. As the ship tilted down and to the left, he skated rapidly forward and banged into the forward bulkhead near the engine-room speaking tube, and grabbed it to keep himself upright. The captain, leading the mate across the deck by half a length, barely managed to sheer away as their courses crossed.

Nick rang the engine room, and the fireman on watch answered. Nick yelled "Send the first to the wheelhouse!" He heard the fireman say something in reply, but he could not understand him.

For a few moments, Nick was occupied, dancing wildly to keep his feet, and could not listen to the tube. He finally regained his balance well enough so that he could yell, "Send the first!" again.

The captain and the mate came skidding by him and the mate yelled, "Get back to the wheel!" Nick looked at him in horror. He had considered himself lucky to make it from the wheel to the speaking tube; the trip back would be worse. The binnacle, standing alone in the middle of the deck, offered a small target. If Nick missed it, he would fetch up against the after bulkhead, with nothing to hold to.

"Hurry up!" the mate yelled. He was making good headway, and had overhauled the captain, who was on his back again.

"I'm plotting a course," Nick said with what dignity he could muster. He decided he would wait until the *Crichton* lay over to port and lifted her prow; that would give him a downhill course to the binnacle, and should allow him to cross the bows of the mate and the captain with room to spare.

Timing himself carefully, he cast off just as the *Andrew Crichton* lifted her bow and began to twist to starboard. Getting off well, he saw that he was on a true course for the binnacle, and had just begun to feel he was making a successful trip when he heard a yell from the mate and saw that he had miscalculated the mate's speed.

They were on a collision course, and as the mate yelled he clipped Nick's feet from under him. Nick felt himself go, and braced for the crash. His first feeling was one of surprise at how soft his landing was. He discovered he had landed amidships of the captain, who was speechless.

Nick made his first trip across the wheelhouse lying face to face with the captain, wondering what to say when the old man recovered his breath. They were traveling headfirst into the bulkhead, and Nick softened the impact by stretching out his hands and fending off.

He felt pleased that he had been able to be useful to the captain, who might otherwise have suffered a nasty blow on the head. He peered down at the captain in the faint light from the binnacle hopefully, hoping he had noticed.

But the captain, if he felt any gratitude, concealed it well. As they started back, Nick tried to keep the captain turning so they would make the far bulkhead first. Unfortunately, the captain had regained his breath now, and was howling words Nick could not understand, and they distracted him so that it was only luck that brought them into the wall broadside instead of head on.

"Get the hell off me!" Captain Haraldsen yelled, and Nick understood him clearly.

Nick abandoned ship smartly.

They sailed precariously back and forth across the wheelhouse several times, waiting helplessly for help from the engine room. The steady howl of the wind and the crashing roar of the waves made conversation impossible, much to Nick's relief. He couldn't think of anything to say.

He gained a lap on the captain, and was leading the mate by half a length before help came. The first assistant opened the door and peered in at last. He could not see very well in the dim light from the binnacle, and he flicked on a pencil flashlight, catching Nick and the mate first in its narrow beam, then picking up the captain. He watched silently for one round trip before he could recover well enough to say something.

"Something wrong?" he asked.

Even over the noise of the gale, Nick could hear the captain's reply. It was a long, detailed examination of the first assistant's inadequacies, ranging over his breeding, abilities as an engineer, and appearance. By the time he had finished, the first had a clear picture of the problem, and left hastily to get help and equipment from below.

Nick and the first mate ran afoul of each other while they waited for his return, and the captain piled into them as they were trying to disentangle themselves. For the next three trips, the three men traveled together, wheeling slowly around as they crossed the deck. It became a matter of concern to Nick to avoid being the prow of this strange vessel as it approached the bulkhead at the end of each trip. The impact with two men behind was much heavier. He scrambled and swam with his hands and legs on the greasy deck well enough to avoid it once, but the captain and mate, working grimly and silently together in what Nick considered an unfair combination of officers against crew, turned him stern to, and made him the equivalent of a human collision mat the rest of the time. By the time the first assistant returned, Nick was bruised and resentful.

The engineer had Stringbeans and a couple of other members of the black gang with him. They carried collision mats and a variety of tools, and used them to make a bridge to the binnacle across the deck. From the security of this dry base, Stringbeans set about fishing for the captain with a boathook while the mate and oiler worked on the hydraulic cylinder.

On his first few casts, Stringbeans managed only to prod the old man in a variety of tender places. He succeeded, at last, in catching him by the belt, and hauled him ashore. He was surprisingly quiet, except for a howl or two when Stringbeans jabbed the tender spots. Nick decided he must be speechless from rage or from being battered against the bulkhead.

Nick waited patiently while Stringbeans, more expert now, snagged the mate by the back of his collar and dragged him to safety. He expected to be rescued immediately, but the first called to Stringbeans for help with the steering gear, and Nick sailed forlornly back and forth for another trip. He called to the small group on the collision mats, but they paid no attention.

It was only when the wheel had been repaired and the ship was answering it again that the mate remembered Nick. When he was hauled to the dry island of mats, it was so that he could go back on wheel duty.

By the time he had wrestled the *Crichton* back on course, the mate had put collision mats in position so that he and the captain could stand at the front of the wheelhouse, surveying the wind and the weather.

Dawn was breaking now, and the seas seemed a bit easier to Nick. He was still resentful because the captain and the mate had made him the buffer in their collisions with the bulkhead, but, by moving his arms and legs cautiously, he found that no damage had been done.

The AB from the eight-to-twelve came up to relieve him,

and Nick gave him the course and started to leave the wheel-house. The old man called to him, and Nick turned.

The old man looked at him solemnly for a moment, then grinned.

"Son, you're as yar a ship as I ever steered," he said. "Especially down by the stern."

10

Despite the delay caused by the bad weather, Nick thought that the *Andrew Crichton* had made the convoy rendezvous in time when she dropped her hook in New York harbor, one of what seemed to be hundreds of ships swinging to anchor there. The mate set anchor watches, which meant that they would be in the harbor for at least twenty-four hours.

The crew went off seat watches as soon as the hook was down, at about eight o'clock in the morning. Nick, Mac, and Heavy were just coming off duty, and the mate knocked them off; then he turned to the other two watches working on deck.

Captain Haraldsen had announced that there would be no shore leave, but Nick, in his capacity as deck delegate, went to see the first mate anyway, and invented a union rule saying that the crew must be granted shore leave if the ship were in port twenty-four hours or more.

The little mate grinned at him and shook his head.

"Look, Nick," he said patiently. "This is my first trip as a chief mate, but I been going to sea for twenty years, give or take a year. There ain't any rule like that."

"Okay," Nick said. "It didn't hurt to try, anyway. Looks like we're going to be here for a while, and I just thought that maybe we could catch a harbor taxi and have a drink or two on shore."

"The old man don't want everybody going ashore and getting smashed and missing sailing time," the mate said. "With all the first trippers we have on board, there must be five or six just waiting for a chance to jump ship anyway."

"Not me," Nick said. "Nor Heavy nor Mac. We're not first trippers, Chief. We figure we've got a bird's nest on the ground on the *Andrew Crichton*. You know we'll be back before sailing time."

"I can't give you a pass, anyway," the mate said. "Captain's orders."

He picked up a pad on his desk and tapped it against the palm of his hand. "It really wouldn't be hard," he said, looking at Nick. "Here's the passes. All I got to do is write them out." He put the passes back on the desk and stood up.

"I got to go up forward and check on the deck gang," he said. "See you later, Nick. I'm sorry."

He left Nick in his cabin, and Nick tore four passes off the pad and took them to the fo'c's'le, where he filled them out for himself, Mac, Heavy, and Stringbeans.

Heavy had showered and shaved and dressed in his shore-going clothes, just in case the captain should change his mind. When Nick showed him the passes, he wanted to leave immediately.

"We have to wait a while," Nick explained. "Don't race your motor, Heavy."

"I can't wait," Heavy said petulantly. "I must of lost twenty pounds eating on this ship. First thing I'm going to do is find me a good place to eat."

"We can't leave until after the old man does," Nick told him. "He has to go ashore for his orders. He said no shore leave. You think we can hail a harbor taxi with him standing on the bridge watching?"

"I'm going to order six fresh eggs over easy and four slices of ham and six pieces of toast buttered with fresh butter," Heavy said blissfully, paying no attention to Nick. "And coffee made out of coffee beans and not boiler scrapings. Then I'm going to eat all of it and start over again."

Mac had listened silently, as usual.

"What time do you think the old man will leave?" he asked now.

"I don't know," Nick said. "They have the captains' meeting in the morning. Seems to me it's usually about ten."

"How about Stringbeans?" Heavy asked. "He coming with us?"

"I got a pass for him," Nick said. "I don't know if he can use it, since he's in the black gang. Maybe he has to have a pass from the chief engineer or the first assistant."

"That ain't possible," Stringbeans said from the doorway. "The chief ain't going to give me one when the captain said no shore leave, and the first assistant must of drunk the cooling system dry. I ain't never seen a man so drunk."

"You might as well try this one, then," Nick said, handing him a pass. "Passes must be the same for the deck gang as for the black gang. Only way you can get in trouble is if we get picked up for something and they check your papers and find out you're an oiler."

"Don't make me no more trouble," Stringbeans said happily. "We're gonna be in so much trouble if they catch us they ain't gonna care whether I sail on deck or below. But they ain't gonna catch us, anyway. They is too many merchant marines in New York right now for four more to make a splash."

"One thing," Nick said. "We got to get back in time. I told the mate we would."

"We'll be back," Mac said.

Heavy got up and went to the small mirror on the inside of his locker door and tied his tie very carefully. He started to waddle out of the fo'c's'le.

"I'm going up on deck and watch to see when the old man goes ashore," he said. "I'll whistle when he leaves."

"Don't let him see you all dressed up," Nick warned. "He'll know something is wrong."

"Don't worry," Heavy said. "I'll keep out of sight."

"You and the Statue of Liberty," Stringbeans said. "You got about the same problem keeping out of sight."

Heavy left, and Nick got a towel and a bar of soap out of his locker.

"We better get ready," he said, and Mac and Stringbeans followed him out of the fo'c's'le.

The head was empty, and they took their time showering and shaving. Nick was beginning to have doubts about the wisdom of going ashore, but he did not see how he could back out now.

He pondered the various penalties if they were caught, and finally decided it could not be too drastic. There was a shortage of merchant seamen, and it seemed unlikely that the authorities would deprive the nation of four for very long, if at all. It might be a long trip and a long time before he could get a drink or a woman, and besides, he needed a haircut.

He clanked back over the steel deck and down the com-

panionway to the fo'c's'le in his wooden shower shoes. Mac
had finished before Nick had, and he was sitting on the edge
of his bunk, talking to Stringbeans, who had dressed himself
up in a junior assistant engineer's uniform with an impressive
array of ribbons over the left breast pocket. One of them was
for service in the Boer War; Stringbeans had bought them at
random in a hock shop in New Orleans, and had no idea what
they stood for. They made a big hit with B girls; Nick wondered briefly if he needed an assortment of his own, but
decided against it.

"The chief give any passes to the black gang?" Nick
asked him.

"Chief wouldn't give hisself a pass for a piece of ass,
even figuring he could use one, which he couldn't at his age,"
Stringbeans said cheerfully. "But I got another pass anyway,
maybe better than the one you give me."

"How did you do that?" Nick asked him.

"Caught the first looking for some more grain alcohol,"
Stringbeans said. "I waited until he had a couple of glasses,
and he didn't know if he was giving me a pass or logging me
for not oiling the main bearings. Prob'ly thought he was logging me."

He tapped his foot impatiently, waiting for Mac and
Nick to finish dressing.

"Besides, I told him it was a emergency," Stringbeans
said. "Said I had to send money to my wife to have a baby
with."

"Don't give yourself a jinx," Mac said. "Maybe she is."

"She ain't gonna have nothing," Stringbeans said. "Leastways as far as I know. I ain't seen my old lady for four years.
She been living down on a bayou fishing for shrimps in her
free time and making time with mens for money. Any time
money changes hands, it's from her to me, not me to her."

Mac had dressed up in a purser's uniform with nearly

as many ribbons as Stringbeans and with two small silver torpedoes over the ribbons. Nick knew that he had earned the torpedoes; Nick himself had the right to wear two. Each torpedo meant that the wearer had had a ship shot out from under him.

Nick wore civilian clothes; he had a purser's uniform, too, but he had not worn it yet, and he felt reluctant to wear it now. A purser's license could be had for the asking. Nick had no ribbons, either; he pinned his two torpedoes to the lapel of his coat, and let it go at that.

He knew that in civilian clothes in New York he might be the target for insults from some of the desk-operating soldiers and sailors who swarmed in the Manhattan bars. Nick knew of no merchant marine bars such as Curly's in New Orleans, but he was not worried. He was surprised to find that he felt proud of the civilian clothes with the two unobtrusive silver torpedoes for decoration.

As he finished dressing, Heavy came in.

"The old man is getting ready," Heavy said. "A boat's coming alongside, and the old man and the chief engineer are waiting. Man, you got to see them. They got more scrambled eggs on their caps than MacArthur."

They followed Heavy out to the dock and watched the tall, angular captain and the short, fat chief engineer board the coast guard cutter that had come alongside to take them to the convoy meeting. They watched until the cutter was lost in the host of ships swinging to anchor in the harbor; then they persuaded a navy signalman to blink for a water taxi.

The gangplank had not been rigged for the short stay in New York, and they had to go over the side to the water taxi on the same swaying rope ladder down which the captain and the engineer had scrambled nimbly. They nearly lost Heavy, who was terrified by rope ladders.

After he had slowly and painfully managed to get halfway down this one, he stopped and refused to go any farther. He could not see below, and he was unable to pull himself back up. He stayed where he was for five minutes, complaining steadily. Finally, Mac, who was waiting impatiently behind him, went down the ladder and stepped on his hands until he had to go on down to keep from falling. He barely made it into the taxi.

By the time they reached shore and paid off the taxi pilot and found a diner to pacify Heavy, it was eleven o'clock. The counterman watched Heavy eat a dozen fresh eggs with rashers of ham and bacon and a pot of coffee, and gave him a wholesale rate out of pure admiration.

"How much money we got?" Stringbeans asked when they left the diner. "I couldn't get no draw from the purser. He said they wasn't no liberty so they wasn't no draw."

They added up their resources, and found that, among them, they possessed a little less than fifty dollars.

"We have to put aside twelve bucks for the taxi back," Nick said. "I'll keep that." They gave Nick the twelve dollars, and then tried to decide what to do with what they had left.

"What we got to do," Stringbeans said, "we got to find a good bar with some rich civilians want to buy war heroes a few drinks."

"Then we got to go uptown," Mac said. "Ain't no good bars nor no rich civilians around here."

"What I would like to find me is a rich female civilian," Heavy said. "One with a taste for a substantial-type man. We going to be a long time on the water."

"Or a lot longer time in it," Stringbeans told him. "You mean, you looking for a woman with a taste for fat boys. A nice skinny, curly-hair merchant marine like me don't have no trouble finding a fine lady, but they ain't that many blubber lovers around."

"Some women purely love a man with some meat on

him." Heavy said. "You can't drive a spike with a tack hammer."

"You hit it enough times, you can," Stringbeans said. He did a little dance on the sidewalk, shaking his shoulders and wiggling his bottom, and a few people stopped to stare at him. "Besides," he said, "I got more like a riveting machine, not no tack hammer."

"Are we going to go or are we going to stand here and entertain the people passing by?" Nick asked impatiently. He did not like the feel of time rushing past.

"Let's go," Mac said. "We ain't got time for no argument about whether women like fat or skinny merchant marines. We got to get out among 'em and give them the opportunity to make their choice—fat, skinny, or suffering with a bad case of the uglies, like me."

"You got to find one like a skinhead," Heavy said as they moved off.

"And there's some of them, too," Mac told him with his catfish grin.

Nick whistled, and a cab pulled to a stop in front of them and they piled in.

"Where to?" the cabbie asked.

"Where the action is," Stringbeans told him. "And the fine ladies."

"There's a house about a mile from here," the driver said. "Cost you ten bucks apiece, but it's strictly high class."

"Not a whorehouse," Nick said. "We want to go to a good hotel bar uptown."

Nick was sitting in the front seat by the driver because Heavy took up so much of the back that Mac and Stringbeans had to sit on the jump seats.

"You name it," the driver said.

"We'll let you pick it," Nick said, "But let's get moving. We don't have too much time."

Thirty minutes later, the cabbie dropped them off in front of a big hotel in the fifties. The bar was a long one, crowded with civilians having their prelunch drinks and service men having drinks.

The four merchant seamen finally found room at one end of the bar, and stood there uncomfortably, waiting for the bartender to notice them. Nick felt a little conspicuous in his civilian clothes. He was the youngest man at the bar out of uniform. A few of the customers looked at them curiously, but he stared back at them, and no one said anything.

The bartender was obviously in no hurry to wait on them. He was wearing a red jacket and a black sash and dress trousers and a supercilious expression, and Nick decided that he felt it beneath his dignity to serve anything less than twelve-year-old Scotch. When he saw the oddly assorted group waiting at the end of the bar, he became very busy serving other customers and washing glasses at the far end of the bar when he had nothing else to do.

Nick began to sweat gently from embarrassment; by now it seemed to him that everyone in the bar was looking at him and talking about his being dressed in civilian clothes.

"Maybe we better get out of here," he said in a low voice to Mac. "I don't think they care much for merchant marines in this bar." Mac was on his left, with Stringbeans and Heavy on his right, near the wall.

"Get out, hell," Mac said in a loud voice, bringing the low hum of conversation in the room to a halt. "What kind of a place is this where four merchant marines just come back from two weeks on a life raft in the North Atlantic can't even get a lousy beer?"

His outburst gained the undivided attention of the rest of the customers, and Nick considered ducking out of sight behind the bar. Mac and Heavy glared at the bartender, and

Stringbeans grinned. The bartender pretended he had an order to fill at the other end of the bar.

"Come on," Nick said, angry now. "Screw them. Let's go."

A small, meticulously dressed man in his early sixties who was standing next to Mac stopped them with a gesture.

"I beg your pardon," he said. "I could not help overhearing this young man's remark. May I be of assistance?"

Before any of them could reply, he called "Charles!" in a quiet voice, and the bartender hurried down to him.

"Yes, sir?" he said, and Nick thought for a moment he would bow and knuckle his forehead, but he managed to restrain himself.

"My friends here are thirsty," the man said. "Will you find out what they would like to have?" He said it coldly, and Charles had four cocktail napkins on the bar so fast it looked like a card trick.

"Put the drinks on my tab," the man said.

"Certainly, Mr. Fitch," Charles said. "What will it be, gentlemen?"

"We can't let you do that," Nick said, and had to bite his tongue to keep from crying out with pain. He sank gently to his knees, wondering if his legs were broken. Mac and Heavy had simultaneously kicked him, one from each side.

"Don't pay no attention to him, Mr. Fitch," Stringbeans said unctuously. "All them days freezing to death on that life raft and losing his uniforms kinda chilled his brain. He ain't been the same since they picked us up."

"How unfortunate," Mr. Fitch said sympathetically. Nick pulled himself erect and tried to figure a way to rub both ankles at once, inconspicuously.

"Are you under medical care?" Mr. Fitch asked him solicitously.

"They ain't nothing they can do," Stringbeans said. "He just gets these sudden spells like, ever' now and then."

"Is it very painful?" Mr. Fitch asked. The people at their end of the bar were listening, and Charles, the bartender, was standing respectfully awaiting their orders, although there were people in the middle of the bar who had called to him. Nick was too embarrassed to say anything.

"It's mostly his feets," Stringbeans explained. "He gets these sudden pains in his feets because the part of his brain connected to his feets got so cold."

"Poor lad," said Mr. Fitch. "Should he be drinking?"

"Only thing in the world that helps him," Heavy said. "Or helps us, either. Warms the brains, and then he forgets how his feet feel."

"Does he drink something special?"

Almost everyone was looking at Nick, and he could feel his face flushing.

"Brandy and sweet," Heavy said promptly.

"Vodka and tonic," Mac said.

"Bourbon and branch," said Stringbeans.

Mr. Fitch and Charles looked startled.

"Which one is it?" Mr. Fitch asked Nick, who managed a sickly grin.

"Scotch and water," he said.

"That's a chaser," Stringbeans said hurriedly. "After all them others."

"He better have them one at a time," Charles put in doubtfully. "Mixing up all those drinks could kill a man."

"Just Scotch and water," Nick said. "You all can drink what you want, but I want a Scotch and water." His ankles throbbed dully, but the attention of the other patrons had drifted away from him, and he felt better, and thought that he needed to protect his interest in Mr. Fitch.

"He must be coming out of it," Mac said, and poked his finger smartly in Nick's eye. Nick started to hit him, then realized that Mac was pretending to examine him.

"His eyeballs are getting better," Mac said seriously to Mr. Fitch. "They get elated when he's having a spell."

"Elated?" asked Mr. Fitch, puzzled.

"You know," Stringbeans said kindly. "Bigger around in the middle."

Nick wiped his eye and took a deep drink from the Scotch and water Charles had placed on the bar in front of him. It was almost pure Scotch, and the pain in his ankles subsided considerably.

A tall, attractive woman in her early forties had moved down the bar to stand next to Mr. Fitch. Nick thought she must be a friend of his, but she paid no attention to Mr. Fitch, and watched Nick steadily and compassionately.

"The poor thing," she said. "He needs care and understanding."

"No, he doesn't," Stringbeans said quickly. "He's very nearly well, lady. Now you take me. I got worse than he has."

"No, he hasn't," Nick said. "I've got the coldest brain known to medical science, madam. Feel my head." He leaned over, and she felt his head, and her hand felt very warm and soft.

"It feels all right," she said.

"That's just on the outside," Nick assured her. "Down inside it's like a bunch of ice cubes. You ask Mac here." He turned to Mac, and saw at once that Mac was not going to be any help.

"He's practically well," Mac said. "This is the first spell he has had in about six months."

"That's a lie," Nick said indignantly. "I've been having spells practically every day."

Mr. Fitch looked puzzled again.

"I thought you fellows were just rescued from a life raft," he said.

"We was," Heavy put in hurriedly. "About three, four days ago. I'm just barely getting my weight back."

"He got his head froze on another trip," Stringbeans said. "Got it stuck in a freezer compartment in the ship's refrigerator."

"I didn't do any such thing," Nick said. He could feel the Scotch taking hold, and he was beginning to believe in his fictitious heroism, and he resented his companions for trying to discount it.

The woman had paid no attention. She continued to watch Nick, and he smiled at her. She seemed to have grown much younger during the course of his Scotch and soda, and he motioned to Charles for another.

"What's your name?" she asked him.

"Nick," he said. "What's yours?"

"Tristiana," she said. "But most of my friends call me Trixie. Or Tricks."

There was an empty stool on the other side of her, and Nick got up and walked around Stringbeans and Mr. Fitch and sat down on it.

"Let me feel your head again," she said, and put her hand on Nick's forehead. She held it there longer this time, and Nick enjoyed it. Finally she took her hand away, and Nick drank from his new drink. It was almost all Scotch again, and Nick nodded approvingly at Charles.

Mac and Stringbeans were watching him enviously, and Nick winked at them. He took another drink of Scotch, and fingered his silver torpedoes thoughtfully, hoping that Tricks would notice them.

"I think your head felt a little colder then," she said. "You must suffer dreadfully." She touched his torpedoes, and he looked down at them modestly.

"What are the little fishes for?" she asked.

"Them's torpedoes," Stringbeans said. "And he only got two. Me, I got three."

She did not look at Stringbeans. "What do they mean?" she asked Nick.

"Oh, it's not so much," Nick said. The Scotch had given him a warm, expansive feeling. "It's just the merchant marine equivalent of the Congressional Medal of Honor for extraordinary bravery above and beyond the call of duty. That's all." He glanced at Mac and Heavy and Stringbeans to see if they would contradict him, but they seemed struck dumb.

"I know," Tricks said understandingly. "You men don't like to talk about it, do you?"

"No," Nick said. He felt not at all reluctant to talk about it at length. "It's little enough." He was not quite sure what he meant by that, but he thought it sounded modest and brave.

"It sure is," Stringbeans broke in. He was beginning to feel his drinks, Nick thought disapprovingly as he drank the rest of his Scotch and waved at Charles. "It's got little it ain't even used yet," Stringbeans went on. "You hardly ever seen anything so little after all that cold water."

"What ever is he talking about?" Tricks said.

"Don't listen to him," Nick told her. "It's big enough."

"I don't understand," she replied. "What is?"

"Never mind," Nick said. "It's just sea talk."

She put her hand on Nick's and shook her head. "You poor thing," she said. "I believe you're getting delirious. You shouldn't be sitting here at a bar. You should be resting comfortably somewhere."

"I have to go back to sea in the morning," Nick said sadly. "The Murmansk run. And you know what that means."

"He ain't got no idea where he's going anymore than we have," Mac said in disgust. "And if he did have, he ain't supposed to blab it about in a bar."

"You can trust me," Tricks said, pressing Nick's hand. "What does that mean?"

"I better not say," Nick said bravely. He drank more Scotch, and realized that he no longer had to order. Charles kept his glass full without being asked. Nick swished the whisky around in his glass, tinkling the ice and staring into it with the air of a man with terrible memories. He sneaked a triumphant glance at the others, all of whom were watching Tricks hungrily.

"If you don't want to talk about it, I understand," she said.

"Don't want to talk about it," Heavy said, and snorted. "Can't shut him up. That's *all* he talks about. Him and his medals."

"No," Nick said, ignoring Heavy. "We try to forget about it while we're ashore. That's why I don't wear my uniform." He rubbed his fingers over his silver torpedoes again, and sighed. "Besides having lost it at sea," he added.

"What did you do to get the torpedoes?" she asked.

"I'd rather not say," Nick told her. "It might sound as if I were bragging when I was just lucky."

Most of the customers had left the bar by now, and it was quiet. Charles and Mr. Fitch and Nick's companions were all listening, and Nick felt a little uncomfortable.

"Don't be modest," she urged him. "Please tell me."

Nick drank off half his Scotch and soda and stared grimly into the glass and shook his head. He was beginning to believe he really had accomplished something memorable by being on two ships that had been torpedoed, although for the life of him he could not remember anything very courageous that he had done.

"Maybe later," he said. "When we are alone, honey."

"You lads are getting behind," Mr. Fitch said to the others. "Order up." They did.

"There he was," Stringbeans said solemnly, "swimming along ahead of the convoy with a knife in his teeth, fighting off submarines."

"And him bareassed," Mac added. "With a full gale blowing and the temperature at thirty below."

"They's never been anything like it," Heavy said. "Man bit the balls right off a shark, too."

"Ain't no wonder he froze his head," Stringbeans said. "Among other things."

"They must be joking," Tricks said, and smiled. She had been drinking vodka Martinis while Nick drank his Scotch, and she seemed a little vague, although much younger and prettier than Nick had thought when he first saw her. He wondered how he could have been so mistaken, and decided that it was the bad light in the bar.

Mr. Fitch, who had matched them drink for drink, also seemed a bit vague, although a charming and friendly gentleman.

"Maybe you fellows are wondering why I bought you these drinks," he said.

"By no means," Nick said magnanimously. "The thought never entered my mind."

"Mine, either," Mac said.

"Me, too," Stringbeans said.

"I'm buying Nick's drinks," Tricks announced. "He's got that cold head, and I feel it is the least I can do."

"Thank you," Nick said.

"Maybe I can help some other way," she said softly, and squeezed his hand again.

"It seems likely," Nick told her.

"I was in the navy," Mr. Fitch said, paying no attention to anyone else. "Three years during the big war. Happiest three years of my life."

"When was the big war?" Mac asked him politely.

"First World War," Mr. Fitch said proudly. "I was a gunner's mate."

"I like gunners, too," Tricks said. She squeezed Nick's knee gently, and he looked at her fondly. She had large blue eyes and black hair with exciting streaks of what must, he decided, be premature gray. "Are you a gunner, dear?"

"I didn't mean that kind of a mate," Mr. Fitch said severely. He was drunk, but it only made him speak more precisely. "I mean I shot guns. . . ."

"I never could understand about that," Tricks said seriously to Nick. She sipped pensively at her drink and stroked Nick's knee dangerously, then peered around him at Mr. Fitch. "What did you do to your gunner?" she asked. "Or him to you? Whichever way it goes."

"I didn't do anything," Mr. Fitch said slowly and clearly. "And he didn't do anything. I mean there wasn't any him *to* do anything. I am not that way. Not at all. Ask Charles."

Everyone looked questioningly at Charles, who was drinking a large glass of whisky himself, and listening. The bar was now empty except for them.

"It's on doctor's advice," Charles said, trying to hide the whisky behind him.

"That's too bad," Tricks said, and patted Mr. Fitch on the hand. "I mean, did the doctor tell you you had to have men? How about the gunner?"

"No, no," Charles said. "The whisky. That was my doctor's idea. He didn't say a word about Mr. Fitch and the gunner. He didn't care about that."

"God damn," Mr. Fitch said. "I never ever had a gunner in my life. I was just a gunner's mate. I was just a hot shell handler."

"Now he's bragging about how good he was," Stringbeans said.

"I got this condition," Charles said. He brought the

whisky out from behind his back and sipped it medicinally, grimacing.

"It must be catching," Mac said. "I think I got the same thing."

"It comes and goes," Charles said. He was tall and portly, with a majestic purple nose that attested to how long and how serious his illness was.

"Tell her, Charles," Mr. Fitch said impatiently. "Tell her about me."

Charles put his drink down, and leaned on the bar with both elbows, then picked up his drink again and took a small sip, forgetting to make a face. He thought for a moment, then began.

"Well," he said slowly, "it all started when I was about fourteen years old, give or take maybe a year or two. I was learning how to be a chicken sexer on a poultry farm south of Abercrombie, Kansas, at the time. . . ."

"Not about you," Mr. Fitch said. "About how I'm not that way."

"How do you sex a chicken?" Tricks asked with interest.

"It ain't easy," Mac said. "First you got to catch one. I know because I was raised on a farm."

"What you do," Charles said, "you take this little bitty baby chicken and you turn it upside down under a strong light—"

"My God!" Tricks exclaimed. "I was married to a chicken sexer for four years and I never knew it!"

"Charles," said Mr. Fitch desperately, "forget the chickens and tell these people how you have seen me in here with one woman after another. You know I'm not like that."

"Lady, as God is my witness, I never seen Mr. Fitch in here with a chicken," Charles said, holding up his right hand. "And I been serving him for ten years, at least."

"He likes gunners," Tricks said, squeezing Nick on the leg so violently that he jumped. "I do, too."

"I seen him in here once with a lieutenant j.g.," Charles said, pouring all a round. "Wasn't any way for me to tell whether he was a gunner or not."

"That was just a friend," Mr. Fitch said. Then, to Tricks, "I don't like gunners, like you. I like girls."

"He called me a gunner, honey," Tricks said to Nick. "Isn't that an insult?"

"You must be a tail gunner," Nick said, and laughed immoderately.

"I didn't call you a gunner," Mr. Fitch said wearily. "What I meant was that I do not like gunners in the same way that you like gunners."

"I should say not," Tricks said indignantly, trying to focus her eyes on Mr. Fitch, and evidently confused. "Turning those poor things upside down in a strong light. I never heard of such a thing except my second husband."

"That was me," Charles said. He broke open a new bottle of whisky and poured some in each glass. Nick wondered how the Scotch and vodka would mix, but he did not think that anyone would notice.

"I was never married to you in my life," Tricks said. "And I ought to know."

"I didn't mean that," Charles said. "I mean about the chicken sexing. That's where I got these terrible headaches that brought on my drinking condition. Squinting at little bitty chicken butts to try to see if they was boys or girls."

"Number two drank a lot," Tricks said thoughtfully. "Maybe that was what caused it, except I never noticed him squinting. Of course, I was hardly in a position to notice if he was squinting or not."

"What difference does it make?" Heavy asked Charles.

"It makes the headaches go away," Charles said.

"I mean with the chickens," Heavy said. "If they is male or female?"

"You must be like Mr. Fitch here," Tricks said. "I personally think it makes a big difference."

"I'm not like that," Mr. Fitch cried hopelessly. Nick thought for a moment he would break into tears, but he controlled himself.

"Roosters can't lay eggs," Charles said to Heavy. "That's the difference."

"I could of told you that without looking at no chicken's butt," Mac said. "I been knowing that all my natural life."

11

When they straggled out of the bar in the early evening, Trixie attached herself firmly to Nick's arm. While the rest of the group waited for a taxi, she tugged Nick around the corner, away from them. She did not have to tug very hard.

"Come on," she said. "You come with me. Let them go."

"They're my buddies," Nick protested, weakly. "We got to get back to the ship together tonight."

"I'll get you back to the ship," Trixie said, snuggling against him. She felt warm and soft against Nick's arm.

He considered the matter briefly, then nodded. His head was swimming from the drinking, but he was not drunk enough to prefer Mac and Heavy to Trixie.

"Where do you want to go?" he asked.

"To my place," she said. "Get a cab."

The cab ride was not a long one, but it established beyond doubt that Trixie's intentions were not honorable. By the time the taxi pulled up in front of a brownstone house in the mid-fifties, Nick and Trixie had developed a firm friendship, and he looked forward to the night with warm anticipation.

"You'll have to let go so I can pay the cab," he told her. She let go reluctantly, and Nick fished in his pocket for the cab fare. He realized then that he still had the get-home money for the rest of the watch, but he did not worry about it. He paid the driver, tipping lavishly, and he and Trixie stood holding on to each other as the cab drove away. An elaborately uniformed doorman regarded them suspiciously for a moment before he recognized Trixie.

"Good evening, Mrs. Romaine," he said obsequiously. "Can I help you?"

"I don't need help, Richard," she said. "My nephew will help me, won't you, Nick?"

"Sure, Aunt Trixie," Nick said. "Anything for Aunt Trixie."

They steered an unsteady course through the door and into the house, and Trixie insisted on helping him take off his peacoat. She seemed determined to take off more, but Nick protected himself when he saw a young maid coming toward them. She looked at him with distaste, and Nick winked. She took Trixie's mink coat and asked her if she would be needed anymore that evening.

"Not at all," Trixie said expansively. "Feel free to leave at any time. Now, for instance."

The maid glanced at Nick again, then turned and left. Trixie took Nick by the arm and led him up a short flight of stairs, into a big, comfortable room complete with a small bar and furnished with soft chairs and a long couch. She sat on the couch and motioned toward the bar.

"Fix us something, honey," she said. Nick moved to the bar and surveyed the array of bottles doubtfully.

"What would you like?" he asked.

"Vodka martini," she told him.

"You better make it simple. I'm not much of a bartender."

"Scotch on the rocks."

Nick poured two glasses of Scotch, found the refrigerator, and added ice cubes. He had begun to sober up a little, and his head hurt. Trixie had begun to age again, but he regarded her with favor as he brought the drinks. She was sitting on the big couch, and she patted the cushion next to her.

He sat down and gave her the drink and she smiled at him. She raised her drink and said, "To us." Nick touched the glass with his, and almost before he could drink, her glass was empty. He started to get up again and fill it, but she pushed him down.

"You rest," she said. "I'll do it."

She brought back two fresh drinks, and seemed surprised that Nick still held the first one.

"Go fast," she said. "Life is short, Nicholas."

He drank quickly, and she sat beside him again and put her glass on the coffee table in front of the couch. Nick put his glass down and took her in his arms, awkwardly. They kissed inaccurately, and Nick caressed her bosom, feeling a formidable structure of what seemed to be steel and stiff fabric.

He slipped his hand around to her back and unzipped her dress and found that the back of the structure was composed of what seemed an endless row of hooks and eyes. Faced with this barrier, he gave up for the moment and returned to his drink.

"Let's talk a while," he said. He had surmounted four-hook brassieres in his time, but this one seemed to be hooked all the way down to her bottom.

"About what?"

"Sex?"

"Why not?" She laughed, and took his hand, placing it casually on her knee. Nick finished his first drink and put it down and picked up the second. He was beginning to feel better, and her knee was smooth and slippery in silk. He slid his hand back and forth on it for a moment.

"Are you married?" she asked, and Nick shook his head. He thought of the question seriously, still moving his hand.

"Once I was," he said. "But it didn't last long."

"Another woman?"

"No," Nick said. "I guess it was the merchant marine. She didn't like it because I liked to go to sea."

He remembered the end of the marriage, and grinned wryly. The girl was one he had gone to school with, and when they were married, it had seemed meant for the ages, but he had grown tired very quickly.

"Didn't she know you were going to sea?" Trixie asked. She seemed really interested, and Nick looked at her with surprise. She looked back seriously, and he decided this meant something to her.

"She knew," he said. "But she didn't know that I liked it. I've thought about it since, because I wanted to figure out what I did wrong. I don't think it would have made much difference to her if I had had another woman. She would have hollered a little, but as long as it was just a one-night stand, she would have got over it."

"Why do you say that?"

"Well," Nick said, "it happened once or twice. She hollered but she got over it. She didn't get over me going to sea."

Trixie sipped at her drink thoughtfully.

"You had to go to sea," she said. "Didn't you?"

"No," Nick replied. "I could have stayed ashore. I had a critical job."

"Why didn't you?"

"I was bored," Nick said. "Up to here." He took his hand off her knee and raised it to his throat. He was beginning to feel good, and Trixie seemed an exceptionally perceptive and sympathetic woman.

"You know?" he asked her.

She nodded.

"Sure," she said. "I know. I had one like you, Nick. Not as young, but the same kind. I told him to get another job or another wife. He was in military intelligence, and he could have stayed home."

"What did he say?"

"The job was more interesting," Trixie said. "That's what he said."

She picked up her drink and finished it and smiled at Nick. He smiled back, and thought to himself that her husband must have been a man. It takes a man to say that, he thought. But it must have been a hell of an interesting job.

Trixie finished her drink and looked at the glass. Nick stood up quickly and took it from her.

"My turn," he said. "Same?"

"Same."

Nick mixed the drinks, and when he returned with them, she had changed her mood. "We're too serious," she said. "Drink up, sailor. Let's have some fun." She pulled Nick down, almost making him spill the drinks, and kissed him enthusiastically.

"Vive the war," she said. "You need a lesson in hooks and eyes."

The lesson went well enough. By the time Nick had reached the last of the hooks and eyes, he could barely see it, but he undid it and sat up triumphantly. He had had three more drinks, and he looked blearily at Trixie.

"All done," he said.

She took off the contraption and scratched her stomach luxuriously. She seemed to have gained weight in the last hour, but to Nick she was beautiful. I always liked a woman with flesh on her, he thought. Trixie had flesh on her.

He took a deep breath, hoping to clear his head, and put his arms around her. She was much warmer outside the armor, and she returned his embrace powerfully. He spilled the drink he had picked up.

"Not in here," she said. "Carry me into the bedroom, Nick."

He stood up, and Trixie lay back on the couch, arranging herself so that she could be picked up. She was wearing a pair of panties and her makeup. Nick bent over to pick her up and put his arms under her shoulders and knees. He started to straighten up, and nothing happened.

"Hurry," she said.

He took a new grip and set himself, and heaved. He got her knees and her shoulders up, but her bottom was still on the couch. He put her down and considered the problem again. Since he could barely keep himself upright, he felt no confidence in his ability to stay on his feet with Trixie in his arms, even if he could lift her.

She looked at him questioningly, and he smiled.

"You're a little slippery," he said, and set himself. He got a firm grip and strained and straightened and felt his knees quiver. "Which way?" he asked. "Turn right out the door and up the stairs," she said. He turned shakily and wavered through the door, and then realized what she had said. The stairs were steep and narrow, and he looked at them hopelessly.

"I don't think you really care," Trixie said. "You're so slow."

"I care," Nick said.

"So hurry."

Nick braced himself and climbed three steps. His legs ached and his lungs burned, and Trixie, who was not really that big, weighed a ton. He stood for a moment and rested, then put his foot on the next step, tentatively. When he shifted his weight to that foot, his knee bent and he lost his balance and fell over backward.

When he sorted himself out again, he was lying at the foot of the stairs with Trixie lying across his midriff. He could not breathe easily, and he was confused. When he worked out what had happened, he said, "I slipped."

Trixie scrambled to her feet and helped him up.

"I forgot your condition," she said contritely. "With the frozen head. You must be weak from exposure."

"That's it," Nick said. "The exposure."

"Poor thing," she said. "Let me help."

Before Nick could do anything, she had scooped him up in her arms and trotted up the stairs. She dumped him unceremoniously on a bed, and smiled down at him.

"There," she said. "Is that better?"

Nick looked at her happily, and smiled.

"Much better," he said. "You're a strong girl."

"You have no idea how strong," she said, and took off her panties.

Things were mixed up for a while after that, and when Nick became fully aware of circumstances, he and Trixie were almost inextricably entangled. He recalled dimly that Trixie had undressed him and that she had initiated a series of unusual and interesting maneuvers, all of them pleasant.

Trixie had pushed twin beds together so that they were

on one big bed and the two of them were lying across it, with the crack where the beds met under Trixie's bottom. Nick was lying on her, breathing heavily and hoping for the best. He had had so much to drink that he was not sure that the best would be adequate, but Trixie was helping him.

She helped enough so that he could make the proper insertion, and he moved gently and steadily, with Trixie meeting each move. He felt warm and happy and in no hurry to bring this to a climax. It would not have helped much if he had been in a hurry.

Trixie cried out, and held him close, and he knew that she had reached a climax, and hoped that she would reach another. He stepped up the pace of his attack, and the beds slid apart.

Nick found his objective a little more distant but not out of reach. He worked away steadily and with pleasure, and the beds separated a little more. To keep from falling, he took one leg out from between Trixie's and put his foot on the floor, and she squeezed her legs together to keep him from escaping.

Unfortunately, she caught some essential equipment between her thigh and Nick's, and he howled.

"Is it good?" she cried in his ear. "Is it that good?"

She squeezed harder, and Nick thought he had been castrated. He tried to lift up and away, but the movement stretched him beyond repair.

"Aaaaaaah!" Nick yelled.

"Me, too!" she cried. "Oh, Nick!"

She relaxed, and Nick extricated himself and climbed painfully back on one of the beds. She followed him and caressed him gently. He winced and crossed his legs.

"Oh, Nick," she said, "that was so good. I loved it when you cried out. Did you feel it that much?"

"Yes," Nick said. "More than you know."

She squeezed him affectionately, and Nick cried silently.

"You're so sensitive," she said. "You react." She squeezed him again, and Nick moaned.

"I'm sleepy," she said, letting go. "Do you mind?"

"No," Nick said. "I'm sleepy too."

She turned on her side and nestled against Nick, and he moved so that she would not come in contact with the sensitive area.

She reached behind her back and tapped him gently there, and he arched his back and stifled a scream.

"You know something?" she asked. "Your wife was a nut. I'd settle for you part of the time. Any part."

"Thanks," Nick said. "I better go."

"Go?"

"I got to get back to the ship," Nick said. "What time is it?"

"I don't know," she said. "Not late." She turned on the light and looked at the clock on the bedside table. "It's only two," she said. "We have time for one more."

Nick scrambled out of bed and found his underwear and started to put them on.

"I'm due," he said. "I got to get back. They're waiting for me."

"Once more," Trixie said, reaching for him. "One more time."

Nick eluded her grasp and pulled his trousers on. He felt a faint ache in his groin, and he was dizzy from whisky, but he kept dressing.

"Next trip," he said. "I'll see you then."

"I hope it's not too long," Trixie said.

"I hope there's something left," Nick told her, and left.

12

Nick found a taxi with no trouble and told the driver to take him to the area where they had come ashore in the morning. He leaned back in the seat and felt himself gently to see if there were any irreparable damages, but aside from a supersensitivity, all seemed well.

He thought back on the afternoon and the night, and felt that it had been well spent. By the time he had arrived at this conclusion, the cab was at the dock and he got out and paid.

Heavy, Mac, and Stringbeans were sitting hunched against the cold, and looked at him balefully.

"Where you been?" Heavy asked. "Banging Miss Money?"

"Miss Money?" Nick said. He had forgotten that Trixie had money. "She wasn't Miss Money. She was a friend. She hurt but she was friendly."

Luckily, they found a water taxi without trouble. They had to wake up the pilot and dicker a while before he agreed to take them to the *Andrew Crichton*. He finally agreed grudgingly for twice his normal fare, and they climbed aboard.

By the time they had located the ship and pulled alongside, it was after three in the morning. Nick hailed the gangway watch and persuaded the seaman to let down a ladder. When it was lowered and secured, Nick paid the taxi pilot and waited while Mac and Stringbeans swarmed up the ladder to the deck.

"All clear," Mac called down. "Come aboard. Hurry up before an officer comes on deck."

Nick went up easily, then looked back down to the water taxi, where Heavy stood looking at the ladder with loathing.

"Come on," Nick said to him. "We can't stay here all night. It's the second's watch, and he may decide to check the deck any minute."

"The old man ain't come back aboard yet," the AB on watch said. "You better get out of sight before he comes alongside."

"Come on," Nick yelled down at Heavy. "The old man is due alongside any minute."

Galvanized into action, Heavy put a tentative foot on the bottom rung of the ladder. "I'm coming," he said querulously. "I just can't make up my mind to get on that little ladder."

He climbed carefully to the gunwale of the taxi, tipping the boat dangerously and making the pilot complain profanely.

Heavy paid no attention to him while he put his other foot on the bottom rung of the ladder. As soon as he was clear of the rail of the taxi, the boat righted itself, and Heavy, having second thoughts about leaving the security of its deck, tried to step back into it, but the pilot opened the throttle and pulled away quickly, leaving the fat man dangling at the end of the ladder, with one foot pawing the air.

He finally got both feet back on the bottom rung and peered down at the black water some six feet below him, cursing the taxi pilot at the top of his voice.

"Shut up and come on board," Nick called down to him. "You're going to wake up the whole ship."

Heavy tried to climb up another rung, but the ladder swayed dangerously and dipped, and he refused to move. He tried again and then stopped, looking up at the deck where Nick, Mac, and Stringbeans and the AB on watch lined the rail peering down at him.

"Don't just stand there," Heavy said. "Haul the ladder up. I can't climb up this God-damn thing."

"I think he's right," Nick said to the others. "No way he can climb the ladder. We better try to haul him up."

It was impossible for all of them to get a purchase on the ladder, and tug as they would, they could not budge it. After hauling, pulling, and grunting for five minutes, they quit trying, and looked over the side at Heavy again.

"You better think of something," the AB on watch said. "Mate told me to keep a sharp eye out for the old man because he's due back on this watch. And there's only about thirty minutes of it left."

"What you all doing up there?" Heavy called. "I can't hang on here all night. I'm getting tired."

"If we don't figure out some way to get him aboard," Mac said, "we're in trouble. If we don't fish him up here before the old man gets back, he'll log us all a month's pay."

"Must be steam on deck," Stringbeans said thoughtfully. "Maybe we could haul him up with a winch."

"Ain't no fair lead over the rail for the ladder," Mac said. "We'd have to rig a boom over the side and bring him up in a bosun's chair."

Heavy was bellowing again from the bottom of the ladder, but they paid no attention.

"That's not a bad idea," Nick said. "Let's get the bosun to break out the gear."

"We can't do that," Mac said. "Boats has a hard on at us already. Maybe we can get into the forepeak and get the gear without waking him up."

Mac went forward to see if the forepeak was open, and Nick leaned over the rail and yelled at Heavy.

"Hang on a little longer," he yelled. "We'll get you up in a few minutes."

"I ain't planning on going for no swim," Heavy said sarcastically. "I'm beginning to like it too much right here on the end of this ladder. You figure you can get me on deck some time before morning?"

Mac returned and said that the forepeak was locked, and Nick relayed the information to Heavy, who called him names. Mac leaned over and told Heavy to be quiet, and explained to him again that the captain was en route and that the mate might come out on deck any minute. Heavy subsided to a loud mutter.

Mac, Nick, Stringbeans, and the AB on watch sat down on the edge of the hatch to try to think of another way to hoist the fat man onto the deck.

"Hey," said the AB on watch suddenly. "I got an idea. They was loading small stores early tonight, and I think the boom is still rigged and there is a cargo net on deck. If they got steam on the winch, you could haul him up in the cargo net."

Nick went over to the winch and cranked it a little, and was pleased to hear the faint hiss of steam in the cylinder. The boom was down, held tight by the cargo hook secured in a shackle. He slacked the line by backing the winch off, and Mac freed the hook. Mac ran out more line so they would have enough slack to rig the boom over the side. All this took about ten minutes, and no one remembered to tell Heavy what they were doing.

When the boom was rigged, they started to secure the cargo net to the hook.

"What the hell's going on up there?" Heavy called plaintively. "I can't hold on much longer."

Nick went to the rail and looked over.

"Don't worry," he said. "We have it all figured out. We're going to haul you up with steam power. We've rigged a boom and we'll bring you aboard in a cargo net."

"Maybe the bosun's chair would have been better," Nick said.

"His ass is too fat for a bosun's chair, anyway," Mac said. "The net is gonna be hard to handle, though. You got to lower him away real easy to the deck because he's gonna be on his back, and he won't be able to break the shock."

"Maybe we could rig a Spanish bowline, and he could slip his legs into the loops," the AB on watch said. "Then he would land feet first."

"Ropes would cut right through the fat," Stringbeans said. "We got to go with the net. Ain't no other way."

"Somebody has to go over the side in it," Mac said. "We got to have some weight to lower away, and we got to have somebody down there to help him get in."

"Not me," Stringbeans said hastily. "I work belowdeck because I don't like being up high."

Finally Mac and Nick flipped a coin, and Mac lost. He climbed into the cargo net, and Nick went to the winch. He moved the handle very gently and picked Mac off the deck, then swung the boom over the side and began to lower away.

Stringbeans stood at the rail giving him directions, and he let Mac down slowly until Stringbeans signaled that he was level with Heavy at the bottom of the ladder, and Nick stopped lowering away. He secured, and went to the rail to watch Mac help Heavy into the cargo net.

Heavy did not care for the arrangement, and wasted precious minutes grumbling about it before he agreed to make an attempt to get in the net.

Mac climbed out of the net onto the ladder above, and held the net steady while the big man tried to get into it. He was tired, and reluctant to take his foot off the ladder.

At last Nick threatened to pull the net up and go to bed and leave Heavy dangling, so Heavy took one foot off the ladder and pawed at the cargo net with it while Mac held him, and Nick and Stringbeans shouted instructions. Heavy finally managed to get his foot over the edge of the sling, and Mac, holding the ladder with one hand, spread the opening of the net with the other hand and his foot.

"Jump," he said to Heavy, and Heavy pulled his foot back.

"I can't even jump on dry land," he said.

Mac hauled the net close to the ladder again and got in it himself, spreading the mouth wide.

"Put your foot out," he said, and Heavy carefully slid his foot over the edge of the net. Mac grabbed it and hauled lustily, and Heavy yelled and came free of the ladder, falling into the bottom of the cargo net with Mac on top of him. The net sagged until it dipped into the icy water, and Heavy howled again.

Mac scrambled to his feet, clambered over the edge of the net and onto the ladder, and went up it to the deck. He joined Nick, Stringbeans, and the AB in looking over the rail. Heavy lay on his back in the bottom of the net, swinging gently back and forth, just brushing the tops of the small waves. He stared back up at them venomously, too angry to talk.

"You handle the winch," Mac said to Nick. "I'll give you the signals."

Nick returned to the winch and kept his eye on Mac, who was leaning over the rail. He was no expert in running a winch because longshoremen did the work of loading and discharging, and the deck gang used winches only to top or cradle the booms. Nick had seldom been a winch operator even during that phase of preparing for sea or port.

Mac raised his arm and called, "Hoist away easy!"

Nervous, Nick opened the throttle too quickly, and Heavy came up out of the water with a rush. Before Nick could slow the machine, he saw Heavy come wailing past the rail in the cargo net, going up like a fat angel in a hurry.

He was high over the rail and near the top of the boom before Nick could stop the winch. Heavy howled all the way up, hanging grimly to the net. When it finally came to rest, swaying wildly, Nick breathed a sigh of relief.

Heavy's cries died out, and the night was quiet as the four men on deck stared thoughtfully up at the cargo net.

"I think he fainted," Mac said. "You took him up pretty fast, Nick. You better lower him away, but take it easy, for God's sake."

"I'm no winchman," Nick said. "But easy it is."

He reversed the winch and misjudged again, and Heavy came down as fast as he had gone up, shouting imprecations as he disappeared over the edge of the rail. His voice faded as he dropped, and stopped with a loud splash. Though Nick reversed the throttle, he judged he must have been too late.

Mac was staring over the side as Nick got the winch stopped, and yelled, "Hoist away! He's awash!"

Nick was sweating now, despite the cold, and he was determined to lift Heavy gently. He cracked steam on the winch as slowly as he could, and was relieved when he saw the tackle take the strain gradually. From the creaking of the gear and the laboring of the winch, he could tell that Heavy was still in the net. In a few moments more, he was sure of it. He could hear the fat man gurgling and cursing and spitting water; he did not sound as though he had been injured.

He kept the winch pulling slowly and steadily until he saw Heavy inching into sight over the rail, dripping water like a beached grampus. Nick set the winch at neutral when Heavy was even with the top of the rail, and went over to help figure out how to get him inboard.

Heavy spat out a mouthful of water, and regarded them balefully through the squares of the netting.

"We could swing the boom in with the winch and lower him to the deck," Stringbeans said, but Nick shook his head.

"It's hard enough for me to take him up or down," he said. "You have to work two winches together to do that."

"Have a meeting," Heavy suggested from the net, where he was swinging gently and dripping water like a small rain cloud. "Don't worry about me. I like it here."

"Tell you what," Mac said. "We'll get some boathooks and start him swinging, and when he swings in over the rail, slack away fast and he'll land on the deck."

"And bust my ass," Heavy put in gloomily.

"Maybe we should put down a couple of mattresses for a landing field," the AB on watch offered.

Stringbeans went to get the mattresses out of their fo'c's'le, and Mac and the AB found boathooks and started Heavy swinging while he complained loudly and steadily. String-beans put the mattresses on deck about where he thought Heavy might land, and Nick went back to the winch.

"Slack off when I holler," Mac said, accidentally poling Heavy in the belly with his boathook.

"I'll try," Nick said doubtfully. He was far from sure of

his ability to handle the winch as delicately as the operation demanded, but he watched carefully as Heavy swung in wider and wider arcs.

Watching Heavy, he was aware of the lights of a small boat approaching in the distance, and wondered if it might be bringing the captain and the chief engineer back.

Distracted, he reacted late when Mac yelled, "Lower away!"

13

By the time Nick slammed the winch handle down to lower Heavy to the deck, the fat man had begun to swing outboard again, and he landed on his bottom on top of the rail, where he teetered precariously for a long moment before sliding slowly overboard. Nick jerked the winch handle to reverse and then to stop, and was relieved not to hear another splash.

He went to the rail and looked down; Heavy was midway between the sea and the deck, bouncing up and down slowly, and cursing.

"Haul him up again," Mac said. "You were a little late then. I'll holler sooner this time so he'll clear the rail on the way in."

Nick hauled Heavy carefully up until he was in position just over the rail again, and Mac and Stringbeans started him swinging.

This time Mac called too quickly. Nick reacted instantly, and Heavy was two feet below the rail on the way back to the water when he swung soggily into the side of the ship. Nick heard a receding series of soft thumps as Heavy descended again while Nick nervously stopped the winch, then wiped the perspiration from his forehead.

"Maybe somebody else ought to run this thing," he suggested.

"You're getting better at it," Mac comforted him. "I'd be worse than you are."

"Don't seem likely," Stringbeans said. "Nobody could."

"Let's try again," Mac said, peering over the rail. He gave Nick the hoist sign, and Nick once more hauled Heavy up to the level of the top of the rail. The fat man was speechless now, whether from anger or from thumping against the side of the ship, Nick could not tell.

Nick left the winch and joined the others at the rail to discuss a new approach. Heavy watched them silently, anger and apprehension twisting his small face."

"What we got to do is get our timing down," Mac said. "I figure a couple of more tries and we'll make it."

"No," Heavy said sadly from the sling. "No. No more tries. Lower me away into the water and I'll try to swim ashore. I can't take no more tries like that last one. There ain't a whole bone left in me."

"Just one more time," Nick assured him. "I think I've got it down pretty well now. The third time is the charm."

"I'm getting out," Heavy said frantically, struggling in the net. They watched him try for a moment, but he was helpless.

"Let's try a hand signal," Mac said. "When I drop my hand, let her go."

Once more Nick made his way back to the winch, and Mac and Stringbeans poked at Heavy with the boathooks until they had him swinging wildly. He had given up protesting, and seemed almost resigned to his fate by now. This time they built up his swing wider than before.

Watching for the hand signal, Nick kept his eye alertly on Mac's raised hand. He heard a call, and slammed the winch handle forward by reflex action before he realized that Mac's hand was still held in the air and the voice had come from over the side.

"Ahoy!" he heard again, and froze.

Heavy disappeared below the rail with a sad cry. Seconds later there was a loud splash, and then a sound like the roar of a wet lion.

"Hoist away!" Mac yelled frantically. Nick was so nervous by now that he jerked the winch handle all the way over, and Heavy shot by the rail, headed aloft at breakneck speed, howling inarticulately. Nick barely had presence of mind left to stop him as he reached the top.

"Avast there!" a voice bellowed from below, and Nick secured the winch and went to the rail. From the top of the boom he could hear a sound that made him think Heavy might be crying, but he had no time to think about Heavy now. When he looked over the rail, he forgot the fat man entirely.

The captain and the chief engineer were in a swamped water taxi, both of them dripping wet. Heavy must have made a hell of a splash, Nick thought abstractedly.

As Nick watched, Captain Haraldsen and the chief came up the ladder rapidly, and when the captain gained the deck, he grabbed Nick by the arm and pointed up at Heavy.

"What is that man doing up there?"

"Where?" Nick said.

The captain pointed again, and Nick looked up at Heavy in surprise.

"Oh," he said foolishly. "You mean him." He felt his reply was somehow inadequate, but he could think of no way to expand upon it.

The captain dropped Nick's arm and turned to Mac.

"You!" he roared. "What in hell is going on here?"

Mac shrugged helplessly and did not answer. Stringbeans had disappeared, and the AB on watch had busied himself hauling up the ladder. Captain Haraldsen glared at Mac for a moment, then turned his attention to Heavy.

"Come down from there!" he yelled. "That's an order!"

Heavy had rolled over to his side during one or another of his quick trips so that now he could look down. If he had been crying, he had quit by now, and he regarded the captain impassively.

"How?" he asked.

Captain Haraldsen considered that for a moment, then turned back to Nick and Mac. "Lower the man to the deck," he said grimly.

"Aye, aye, sir," Nick answered sadly, and returned to the winch, an instrument he had begun to regard with horror and distrust. He had decided long since that it operated on a will or a whim of its own and that if he ever succeeded in controlling it, it would be with the consent of the winch itself.

He pushed the handle forward very slowly, and was pleasantly surprised when Heavy began a measured descent. When he was at his familiar station a couple of feet over the rail, Nick stopped him.

The captain eyed Heavy distastefully for a while as he considered the problem of bringing him inboard; then he said,

"Get him swinging, and lower away when he swings inboard far enough."

"They been trying that," Heavy said hastily. "It don't work."

"We just missed a couple times," Mac explained. "I think we can do it now."

"Try it," the captain barked, ignoring Heavy's wail of dismay.

Heavy tried to fend off the boathooks as well as he could, and the captain said: "Lay off that. They're trying to help you."

"No," Heavy said. "They like to kill me three times already"

"You mean when you fell in the water?" the captain asked.

"That was the third time," Heavy said.

"Avast heaving," the captain said to Mac and the AB on watch. "I'll think of something else."

He thought briefly, then turned to Mac. "Call the watch below," he said. "Get the bosun on deck first."

"Sir," said Heavy tentatively.

"What are you doing in the cargo net anyway?" the captain asked Heavy.

"It wasn't my idea," Heavy said defensively. "They thought it up."

"What were you doing at the top of the boom?" the captain persisted.

"I cried a lot," Heavy said.

"Whose idea was this?" Haraldsen asked, looking at Nick.

"We had to get him on board somehow," Nick said. "He couldn't climb the ladder."

"Sir," Heavy said again, "what I wanted to ask you was,

can you just lower me into the water, and I'll swim ashore?"

"You signed on for a full trip," Captain Haraldsen said sternly. "And by God you're going to make it if you have to stay in that sling all the way."

The bosun shambled out on deck and looked at Heavy swinging gently just off the port beam, and scratched his bald head in surprise.

"It's overtime taking on cargo this late," he told the captain.

"That's not cargo!" the captain snapped.

The bosun inspected the sling more closely, and recognized Heavy.

"Git out of there," he said. "Step lively."

"Up yours," Heavy said to the bosun, and made a vulgar gesture with his free hand.

The bosun considered this suggestion for a second, then overlooked it and studied the situation.

"Swing him back and forth and lower away when he comes in over the rail," he said brightly at last. No one said anything to that. The rest of the deck gang had assembled by now, yawning and scratching and looking curiously at Heavy.

"Break out a block and tackle," the captain said to the bosun, who relayed the order and gave an ordinary seaman his keys to the forepeak. The sleepy ordinary started slowly forward.

"Step lively!" the captain roared, and the ordinary sprinted up the deck as everyone jumped.

When he had returned at a trot with the block and tackle, everyone looked questioningly at the skipper.

"Come on, come on," he said irritably. "Secure one end of the block and tackle to the cargo net and the other end to the hatch coaming. We'll haul him inboard with Norwegian steam, then lower away when he's over the deck."

When the tackle was in place, several members of the

crew tailed on to the line and slowly hauled Heavy in over the side. They held it taut while Nick lowered away; unfortunately, he miscalculated again, and Heavy swung too far inboard to land on the mattress. He thumped to the bare steel deck and lay there, tangled in the netting and staring up at the sky.

The captain and the crew stood in a loose circle looking down at him.

"Are you all right?" the captain asked finally, and Heavy turned his head slowly to look up at the old man.

"Oh, yes," he said gently. "Yes, indeed. I'm fine. Nice and clean, sir. From being rinsed in the sea."

"I think he's out of his head," the captain said. "Roust out the purser to come have a look at him."

Heavy rolled heavily over to his belly and slowly disentangled himself from the cargo net. It took him a long time. When he was clear, Nick and Mac helped him to his feet.

"Knock off everyone but the watch on deck," the captain said to the bosun. "Did you send for the purser?"

"I'm okay," Heavy said hastily. The purser's remedy for any ailment from a cold to a broken leg was a shot of penicillin, administered with a horse needle. "I don't need the purser."

Nick and Mac started to help Heavy to their fo'c's'le, but Captain Haraldsen stopped them.

"Report to me in the morning," he said wearily. "I don't even want to know what happened here tonight, but I have to enter something in the log."

14

After listening to their explanations in the morning, the captain logged Mac and Nick each a week's pay. It was not a severe penalty, Nick thought, considering everything. They had kept the mate out of the story, maintaining they had hitched a ride ashore without passes. The captain said that Heavy had been through enough without being logged, and let him off.

Nick and Mac considered this an injustice, since Heavy had been responsible for their being caught, but they said nothing about that to the old man. They expressed their point of view angrily to the fat man, but he did not seem unduly concerned. He was more worried about beginning his own investigation into the loss of his watches.

The *Andrew Crichton* made rendezvous with the other ships in the convoy in midmorning. It was a vast, slow convoy group, ten ships deep and eleven across. The *Crichton* was the lead ship in the seventh column.

It was not an enviable place to be, and Nick wished that they could have been stationed somewhere near the middle of the big square of ships. When submarines hit a convoy, they nibbled at the edges. There was another Liberty to starboard of the *Crichton*, and a C-2 to port, with a tanker aft. Dead ahead were the open sea and the escort ships, tirelessly circling the slow merchantmen. And, Nick thought grimly, the submarines.

It took all of the rest of the day for the convoy alignment to be squared away, with every ship maintaining proper intervals fore and aft and on the port and starboard beams. When Nick, Mac, and Heavy finally went off watch, they turned to on deck to finish battening down for sea. Heavy moved slowly and groaned loudly, to the disgust of the bosun.

They stowed loose gear and tied down whatever could not be stowed below. The North Atlantic with winter coming on would be rough cruise. By the time the four-to-eight went below after standing their evening watch, all of them were exhausted.

They trooped silently into the messroom to eat, and Stringbeans came in a little later, as red-eyed and weary as the rest of them.

"Where the hell did you go last night?" Mac asked him. "You popped out of sight like a chipmunk down a hole when the old man came aboard."

"I had to go on watch," Stringbeans said virtuously. "Besides, they wasn't no good I could do, anyways."

The ship was beginning to roll a little as the wind freshened, but not even Heavy complained. When they hit their bunks, they slept like the dead until they were called for the morning watch.

They dressed slowly and painfully and went for the pre-watch coffee. As he sipped the bitter brew, Nick reflected that it would probably be sixteen days or more before they saw land again. In a convoy as big as this one, the speed would be held to a maximum of eight knots. He counted the thumps of the big engines, and figured the Liberty was turning eighty-two revolutions per minute, which confirmed his estimate of an eight-knot convoy.

He wondered briefly what their destination would be, but it did not make a great deal of difference. The fo'c's'les had not been insulated, so it probably was not Murmansk. It could be anywhere from Liverpool and Manchester to Le Havre or Glasgow. Nick said a private prayer for Le Havre, but he doubted that the Lord would consider his reasons for preferring that port to be religious ones.

He finished his coffee and went up to the bridge to relieve the wheel. Mac was on lookout in the bow, and Heavy was standing by in the messroom.

Nick took the course from the twelve-to-four AB on the wheel, and spent the next hour and twenty minutes trying to stay wide enough awake to keep the compass needle reasonably steady on the course. The captain had decided that Heavy was capable of standing wheel watches at sea, so the watch could be split three ways—an hour and twenty minutes at the wheel, the same amount of time at lookout and on standby. On standby Nick hoped that he might take a nap in the messroom. It seemed unlikely that the mate would require the watch below to work overtime on deck. The ship was secured and ready for sea.

Although it was only a few minutes after four in the morning, Captain Haraldsen was awake and in the wheelhouse. Nick knew he had been awake all night, and he marveled at the old man's stamina. Later in the trip, when the days and nights had settled into routine, Nick knew that he would sleep at night, but this had been thee first full night in convoy, and the captain was making sure that his mates were capable of handling their watches and keeping convoy station.

The tall, gaunt old Norwegian stood talking quietly to the first mate for most of Nick's watch. Occasionally he would wander out onto the wing of the bridge and peer into the darkness, trying to determine if the *Andrew Crichton* was maintaining a proper interval between the two ships on the beams and the tanker dead astern. Sometimes the mate went with him, but more often he stayed behind, out of the biting cold and the wind.

Once, when he was sure the old man was out of earshot, the mate came over to the wheel and asked Nick, "He want to know where you got your passes."

"We told him we didn't have passes," Nick said. "He was pretty good about the whole thing."

"Good," the mate said. "Come by my cabin when we get off watch. I got a couple of bottles stashed."

"Fine," Nick said. Ordinarily he would not have relished the thought of a drink at eight in the morning, but he reflected that things were different at sea. If there is anything available to drink, you drink it, no matter what time of day.

The mate fell silent as Captain Haraldsen returned from his trip to the wing of the bridge, and Nick went back to fighting his growing tendency to close his eyes.

Other than his fight against sleep, Nick found the wheel watch an easy one. The ship was pitching a little, but he had no problem holding her on course, and when Heavy came up to relieve the wheel, Nick had the *Andrew Crichton* dead on. The captain had retired to his cabin to snatch a few moments' sleep, and he returned just as Heavy took over. He sighed gustily and shook his head.

Leaving the wheelhouse, Nick felt his way along the deck in the dark, going forward to relieve Mac, who was standing lookout on the bow. Mac was hunched against the cold, whistling tunelessly between his teeth, and he was pleased to see Nick.

"Cold as a well digger's ass in Alaska," he said cheerfully enough. "But they's one good thing about being lead ship. You don't got to strain your eyeballs looking for a fog buoy in dirty weather."

"Forepeak open?" Nick asked hopefully.

"I ain't tried it," Mac told him. "Ain't been quite that cold yet."

Sometimes, when the weather was bitter and black enough, Nick would duck down into the forepeak for a few minutes to get out of the wind and the spray. He could not see anything from down there, but he could not see anything from his station on the bow, either, especially in the lead ship.

Mac scuttled aft along the deck for his standby trick in the messroom, and Nick tried the manhole cover leading down into the forepeak, and was happy to find it open. He let it down again and went into the vee where the rails came together in the prow of the ship. He strained his eyes looking into the dark ahead, but he could not see anything. The only ships ahead of the *Crichton* would be escorts, and they patrolled the fringes of the big block of ships, not holding any particular station.

Back in the body of the convoy, Nick would have had to keep a sharp lookout for fog buoys on a dark or foggy night when each ship would trail a buoy three hundred feet astern as a warning to the ship following. The buoy kicked up a wide white wake the lookout could see when his ship rode up on it, and he could warn the bridge that they were closing.

The three-hundred-foot warning gave the mate on watch time to reduce speed and drop back, but lookout could be nerve-racking duty in a heavy fog on a black night when the man on watch strained to pick up the telltale feather of white in the blackness ahead.

Nick grinned wryly to himself. It was small consolation thinking that he would have no fog buoys to look for on this trip. The lead ship looked for submarines, and the submarines never trailed identification.

It was cold on the bow, but Nick knew it would get much colder. In a peacoat and long underwear and rain gear, he was warm enough. He wondered how long it would be before the increasing cold would force him to wear the rubberized survival suit over the rest of his clothes. Sometimes, on the North Atlantic, the survival suit, designed to save lives if merchant seamen were torpedoed and had to take to the bitter cold of the water, was necessary to keep from freezing during the short hour and twenty minutes on lookout, especially in the bow with seas breaking over.

Now Nick leaned on the rail and listened to the sounds of the ship in the night. The bow lifted slowly and gently, and dropped with a faint hissing noise, and all that Nick could see was the white of the bow wave curling and spreading away from the *Crichton*'s forefoot.

The sound of the water slipping away on each side of the hull was a steady *shush, shush,* with now and then a quiet splashing when a wave broke against the side, and always the regular thump of the engine, a little faster than Nick's heartbeat.

A bigger wave hit solidly, the ship shuddered slightly, and Nick could hear a subdued clanking from the chain locker. There were faint creakings from the rigging, and the thrum of the wind, but no human sounds at all.

Watching and listening, Nick tried to calculate how many men were in the ships of the convoy and its escort. The crew of a freighter, including officers, men, and gun crew, would go about seventy-five or eighty, he thought. Multiply that by a hundred and ten, the number of ships in the freighter convoy, and it came out something between nine and ten thousand.

Maybe two thousand more men in the escorts, if that many. Say, roughly, twelve thousand men, all on the seas in the blackness around him. Nick was not sure about the escort. Many of the escort vessels were Canadian destroyers, old United States World War I four-stackers, and some were corvettes. He did know how many of them there were or what their crew complements were. The four-stackers probably carried about a hundred and fifty, the corvettes a lot less.

Lost in thought, he was surprised when he heard Heavy stumbling and cursing as he made his way forward to take over the lookout. Nick was almost sorry to hear him coming. Solitude was a rare luxury at sea.

Nick went back to the midship house and the light and warmth of the messroom and shed his rain gear and peacoat. The messroom was empty, and Nick drew a cup of hot coffee. and nursed it between his bare hands, trying to warm them. He drank it quickly, made himself a sandwich from the night lunch, drew another cup of coffee, and settled down to enjoy his snack slowly.

He finished the sandwich and made another, thinking that then he wouldn't be hungry when he went off watch in a little more than an hour, and he could go straight to bed and not waste sacktime eating breakfast.

He ate the second sandwich with a third cup of coffee, reading a paperback book someone had left in the messroom. He was surprised when the sleepy messboy reminded him that it was time to call the eight-to-twelve.

Nick walked along the passageway to the eight-to-twelve fo'c's'le, awakened the three men, then climbed to the boat deck and yelled to awaken the third mate. It was turning light now, and he went back to the messroom and had another cup of coffee. It had been a good watch, with no bad weather and no submarine scares.

It was the end of a summer in which there had been surprisingly little submarine activity on the North Atlantic, as a matter of fact. Nick thought about this for a while, and decided that either the Allied antisubmarine warfare had wiped out most of them or they had retired to lick their wounds and regroup. He hoped that it was the first.

As the trip wore on, the days fell into their familiar pattern, and the routine watches passed as regularly as the hourly ringing of the ship's bell. Nick stood his wheel, lookout, and standby, and spent eight hours on watch below. On one watch below, he slept; on the other, he tried to kill time in a variety of ways.

From his previous trips to sea, he knew that time on the second watch below was hard to kill. He usually slept during the day because he was sleepy when he went off watch at eight in the morning and not when he came off the evening watch. After the evening watch, he sat up in the messroom playing cards until no one was left to play with; then he retired to his fo'c's'le.

He read novels, biographies, histories, and, in desperation after he had exhausted the limited resources of the meager ship's library, a pamphlet on how to cure wheat rust in the Midwest. The library was as spotty as it was limited, and he had not taken time to pick up books of his own as he usually did before shipping out.

The weather grew worse as the convoy steamed slowly along the great-circle route by the coast of Greenland on the way to England. It was as stormy as only the North Atlantic can be in the winter.

Now, on lookout in the bow. Nick's concern was more for icebergs than for submarines. The bergs seldom drifted this far south so early, but occasionally a monster came down into the sea-lanes. The icebergs were more dangerous than a torpedo.

Nick wore a face mask to save his face from freezing. The cold had grown almost unbearable, and without the mask he could not have stood it in the bow with seas sending spray over him regularly. The water froze as it hit the deck, and the upperworks of the ship were encased in a shining sheet of ice.

The moisture from his breath froze the mouthpiece of the face mask to his lips so that when he returned to the mess-room, it was necessary to wait a few minutes for the mask to thaw so he could take it off without taking skin and lips with it. It was a typical North Atlantic winter passage.

The chief mate had proved to be a good head, as Mac had predicted. He kept a supply of whiskey in a drawer under his bunk, and, more often than not, at the end of the morning watch he would invite Nick in, and they would share a drink or two while they warmed up.

"How can you beat this?" he asked Nick one morning. They were drinking the whiskey out of water tumblers, the way the first assistant drank his grain alcohol.

"You're at sea a week, two weeks," the mate went on. "Maybe more on a long run. In peacetime, you can pick a run you like, and stay on it: Europe, the Near East, Japan, China, South America. Good food, good-enough pay. And no responsibility in port. All the girls you want; you see them for a while, bang 'em, then good-bye, good luck, and you're at sea, and you'll probably never see that one again. Sailors don't have a girl in every port, Nick. Not smart sailors. Why buy a cow when milk's so cheap? We usually never go back to the same girl."

Over a second whiskey, it sounded good to Nick. Even during the war, he thought, it sounded good. Every trip was a separate segment of life, complete in itself, with a beginning, a middle, and an end, and, one way or another, some kind of meaning. You went out, made port, raised hell, came back to another port and raised some more hell. No tomorrows, and something to remember about the yesterdays. All you had to worry about were torpedoes and air attack, but even the danger added a spice to life.

"Maybe I'll stay with it," Nick said.

"Do that," the mate said. "Meantime, if you want to borrow any books on navigation or seamanship, I have lots of them."

Nick did not borrow the books then, but he did later. He had always hidden a faint sense of shame for being in the merchant marine, feeling that it would have been more honorable to join one of the services, but the only service he cared about he could not join at twenty-eight. He had been too old for the air force. Lately the sense of shame had left him.

"This has got to be the easiest trip we ever made," Mac said to him one afternoon as they played gin in the messroom. "Not only we ain't had no sub alarms; we ain't even had no excitement on board. I thought the bosun was gonna give us a hard time, but they ain't no way he can for the four-to-eight."

"Gin," Nick said, laying down his cards. "Don't give us a jinx. Knock on wood."

"I done that while I was talking," Mac told him. "Trip ain't over yet."

"I better go get my gear on," Nick said. "I got first lookout. You on standby?"

"That's right," Mac said. "You got last wheel; Heavy's last standby."

Heavy came in and sat down with a cup of coffee. He had completely recovered from his experience in the cargo net, and was in as good a mood as was possible for him.

"I wish we was on the eight-to-twelve," he said, sipping his coffee. "That third look like a nice man. Nice and fat and cheerful, and he got some understanding for the problems of a man carrying meat on him. He seem like a very good-natured man."

"He seems that way," Nick agreed. The third was a roly-poly, rosy-cheeked young man, fresh out of merchant marine officers' school, anxious to please and easy on his watch.

"No trouble to call," Mac said. "Ever' time I go to call him for his watch, he's reading navigation books or studying something else."

"He's trying to get ready to sit for his second's papers," Nick said. "He wants to be ready for the exams when he gets in enough time sailing third."

"He's got lots of time to study, then," Mac said. "I figure this has to be his first trip as a third."

"Must be," Heavy said. "The guys on the eight-to-twelve like him. He acts like he ought to apologize when he asks them to do something. I ain't never heard of him raising hell if they screw up. And I seen the old man eat him out the other day because his watch fouled up the lifeboat check, and he didn't say nothing to them."

"He don't like to be touched when he's asleep," Mac said. "His ordinary told me when they had to wake him up in port, they hollered. He told them not to wake him up touching him. He's got some kind of thing about it."

"He's safe from me," Heavy said. "I ain't about to touch him."

Nick left to put on his rain gear. The weather was gray with a strong, cold wind and a driving rain, and he was glad to come back to the messroom after he finished his trick as lookout. He spent his hour and twenty minutes on standby in the messroom, reading.

When he took the wheel from Mac, the captain was in

the chart room with the mate, drinking coffee. Darkness was beginning to turn to light as Nick neared the end of his wheel watch and he was sleepy and anxious to go below.

The ship's clock struck eight bells, and Nick wondered what had happened to his relief. The first and the captain were still in the chart room, and the first came out and looked at the clock.

"You seen the third?" he asked. Nick shook his head.

"First time he didn't come on the bridge early," the mate said. "I wonder if anything is wrong with him."

Heavy must have fallen asleep and forgotten to call the watch, Nick thought. It would not be the first time. Nick felt happy that he was not freezing to death on lookout in the bow.

The captain came out of the chart room with a cup of hot black coffee and walked to the front of the wheelhouse, staring out at the unending vastness of tumbling gray water. Far ahead, Nick could see a corvette kicking its heels in the rough seas.

Heavy came in, grumbling to himself.

"I can't wake up the third," he told the first mate. "First time I ever went to his cabin when he wasn't up already. He's sleeping like there ain't no more watches."

"I'll get him up," the captain said. "You stay on the bridge, first. I'll be back when the course change comes up."

He motioned to Heavy to follow him, and left the wheelhouse. The mate waited until he had left, then poured coffee for Nick and himself from the pot the saloon messboy had left in the chart room. He often did this when he and Nick were alone in the wheelhouse; the captain did not approve of the quartermaster drinking coffee while he was standing his watch. In most weather, though, Nick could steer well enough with one hand, and the coffee was welcome on a long watch.

"Captain's got his ass on his shoulder," the first said. "Third relieves me early every watch for two weeks, and one day he sleeps in a few minutes and catches the old man mad at the world. He'll probably get logged."

"Wonder how he happened to sleep late," Nick said, and yawned.

"He stood the second's watch," the mate said. "Second got involved with a bottle of whiskey, and the third stood his watch so the old man wouldn't know. Third's gonna be a good man to ship with."

Nick started to answer him, but before he could, the door to the wheelhouse banged open noisily, and the captain came through it running at a full gallop. He looked at Nick and the first mate as he shot through the room and out onto the boat deck, but he didn't say anything. The third came after him before Nick or the first could move, waving a long flashlight and making futile swings at the captain.

The captain and the third disappeared through the door to the deck, and the mate turned to Nick to say something; but just then Heavy lumbered through the aft door at an elephantine trot, waddled through the wheelhouse and out to the deck in the wake of the captain and the third mate.

"What the hell was all that?" the mate asked Nick.

Nick was still speechless with surprise, and could only shrug. The eight-to-twelve AB came into the wheelhouse to relieve him, and Nick automatically gave him the course. Instead of leaving, Nick waited for the first mate, who had gone into the chart room. Nick wanted to find out, if possible, what was going on, and he wanted to be available should the first invite him to have a drink.

He looked in the chart room. The first had just finished charting the change of course.

"I better see what's happening," he said. He came out of the chart room and started out the aft door to the wheelhouse leading into the midship house. Just before he reached the door, the captain came through again, puffing like a diesel engine, but maintaining his two-length lead over the third mate.

The first skipped aside just in time, and ducked one of the third's wild swings with the flashlight. The captain said something indistinguishable as he went by; but the third, who was panting heavily and seemed to be in a trance, trundled by without a word.

The first watched them skid around the corner and sail out the door to the deck again, and started to follow them, then stopped.

"What did he say?" he asked Nick.

"Sounded like 'Arrrgh.'"

The first considered that for a moment, then started back through the aft door. He listened intently for a moment before he opened it.

"Sounds like they're going around the starboard side of the midship house on the boat deck," he said. "Maybe I can cut them off."

He opened the aft door just in time for Heavy to come through at a slow lope and knock him flat. Heavy had lost a good deal of ground on the last lap, but he did not stop. He went on through the wheelhouse and out to the deck, and just as the mate was climbing to his feet, Captain Haraldsen and the third mate fell on him.

The first mate struggled to get to his feet, but Captain Haraldsen and the third were too exhausted to move. Nick stood and watched for a moment, then prudently took the flashlight from the limp hand of the third. He could hear Heavy coming around again, pounding heavily along the passageway just outside the wheelhouse. Nick called out a warning, but Heavy was too tired or too intent to hear him.

He came through the door in a slow, dogged trot, and collapsed on top of the heap while Nick and the AB on watch looked on in amazement. The first mate had quit struggling and was lying quietly, waiting for the pile to be taken off him. With the captain directly on top of him, he couldn't take any drastic means to get free.

Nick could think of nothing to do, so he took another sip of coffee. The captain, who was third from the top in the heap, twisted his head, and tried to say something, but he was breathless from his long run and he had the more than considerable weight of Heavy and the third mate on him.

The third mate, just under the top layer, which consisted of Heavy, began to squirm. To Nick, he looked like a man awakening from a nightmare. With Heavy spread-eagled over him, he had small chance of working clear.

Nick considered this complicated problem, and took another sip of coffee. He supposed, by strict protocol, he could somehow extricate the captain first, since he clearly had seniority and rank. But with the third and Heavy on top of him, he was almost invisible, and certainly inextricable. The first mate came second in precedence but last in possibility, since he was the bottom layer.

Finally the captain got his breath back, or enough of it to make himself understood.

"Get them off me," he squeaked. Though he tried to shout, he could muster little more than a high-pitched whisper.

"Aye, aye, sir," Nick said smartly. Though he was off watch, he felt that this duty came under the head of deck work and that he could logically put in for overtime. He grabbed Heavy by the arm and heaved strongly, but he did not manage to move him appreciably. Heavy himself was too tired to help. He was as limp as a giant jellyfish, breathing stertorously and moaning between breaths.

"Lend him a hand, Quartermaster," the captain said, his voice a trifle stronger. The AB on the wheel looked at him doubtfully.

"Me?" he asked, looking around.

"Who else?" said the third, who seemed almost completely recovered.

"I'm on the wheel, sir," the AB said. "At school they said never to abandon the wheel without relief."

"God-damn it, turn to!" the captain shouted in a hoarse whisper. It was the first time Nick had ever heard anyone manage to do such a thing.

The AB let go of the wheel and came over, and he and Nick rolled Heavy off the top of the pile. Then they helped the third mate to his feet, although he needed little help. He scrambled up as quickly as a fat cat and turned to help Captain Haraldsen, but the captain brushed him off.

He got to his feet without assistance and looked down at the first, who seemed, to Nick, alarmingly flat.

"What kind of ship is this?" the captain asked him.

The first looked at him speechlessly and made a few feeble movements as Nick helped him to his feet. He was wobbly for a while, but he recovered eventually and shook off Nick's supporting arm.

"I don't know," the first said cleverly.

Captain Haraldsen started to say something to him, then noticed Nick and Heavy listening. He glanced at Nick and looked at Heavy long and sorrowfully.

"You two lay below," he said. As they turned to leave, the captain said, "You too," and the mate followed them.

"What happened?" Nick asked Heavy when they had reached the messroom.

"I couldn't wake the third up," Heavy said. "I remembered that his ordinary said not to touch him, so I hollered at him for a while; then I went up to get the first to wake him up."

"I know that part," Nick said. "Then the old man went down with you to get him out of his bunk."

"That's right," Heavy said. "We went into the third's

cabin, and the old man hollered, 'Get your butt out of that bunk, you ninety-day wonder!' but the third, he didn't even twitch."

"Then what?" Nick asked, when Heavy stopped.

"It got kind of confused after that," Heavy said. "The old man hollered 'Turn to!' a couple of times real loud, but the third just snored louder, and the old man got madder and madder. So before I could tell him not to, he hauled off and slapped the third across the face about three times, and the third come out of his bunk like he was crazy. He grabbed a flashlight long as my arm out from under his pillow and took a swing at the old man with it. He missed, and the old man backed off; but the third took after him and took another swing, and missed."

Nick waited impatiently while Heavy drank coffee.

"So what next?" he asked finally.

"Well, the old man ducked, and jumped out of the cabin," Heavy said, putting down his coffee. "The third went out after him. I tried to get out at the same time, and me and the third got stuck or he might of caught the old man right away. The old man got a good start on him."

"So why did you chase after them?" Nick asked curiously.

"I wanted to see if the third caught him," Heavy said. "Never saw a man with a worse swing since a buddy of mine used to play third base in the Texas League. Then after a while the old man come up behind me because he was running faster and the third behind him, and I had to keep going to stay out of the way."

The ordinary on the eight-to-twelve was on standby, and he had listened with interest to Heavy's story.

"The old man never should of hit him," he said, disapprovingly. "The third mate told us not to do that to wake him up."

"What makes him like that?" Nick asked.

"I don't know," the ordinary said. "But he said that if you touch him, he gets up swinging and keeps going until something stops him. I guess he was right."

"What does he keep a flashlight under his pillow for?" Nick asked. "He's got a light in his room."

"He's afraid it might go out," the ordinary said. "He's afraid of the dark."

15

The *Andrew Crichton* steamed into the harbor at Liverpool three days later. Liverpool, as Nick remembered it, was a dirty city lying untidily on the banks of the river Clyde like a brown blight flawing the green countryside around it. You have to be at sea on the North Atlantic a long time before Liverpool is an attractive port, Nick thought as two tugs nudged the ship to its dock.

When the *Crichton* finally came to rest, the deck gang secured the ship, put rat guards on the shore lines, and rigged the gangplank. Nick, Mac, and Heavy retired to the head and showered, then dressed and prepared to go ashore. Mac was adjusting the ribbons on his uniform when the bosun came by and looked in the fo'c's'le.

"Where you going?" he asked.

"Ashore," Mac said.

"You got to turn to," the bosun told him. "It's four bells in the morning watch."

"What time is that?" Nick asked the bosun, because he knew it would irritate him.

"Ten o'clock," the bosun said. "Deck gang has got to work on deck until two bells."

"What time is two bells?" Nick asked, because he did not know.

"Five in the afternoon," the bosun said angrily.

"Doing what?" Mac asked him.

"Got to chip and scrape and red-lead and paint," the bald-headed old man told him, grinning a malevolent, toothless grin. "And I personal am going to see you get logged if you fuck off."

"We been seventeen days at sea," Mac said, pushing the bosun aside. He gave the bosun a detailed description of where he could put the logbook, sideways, and Nick and Heavy followed him ashore.

Liverpool offered little diversion during the daylight hours. But anything was better than chipping and scraping and red-leading over the side of the ship.

Nick, Mac, Stringbeans, and Heavy stopped twice and ate fish-and-chips and went into a Salvation Army canteen and had free doughnuts and coffee. Heavy insisted that they go back for seconds, but by then the Salvation Army people had recognized them as merchant seamen and would not serve them, so they went back out to the street.

It was late afternoon, dark and cold, before they found a bar and pushed in through the blackout curtains. The bar was not far from the dock area, and it was crowded and warm. Most of the customers were men from the English mercantile navy.

Nick led the way as they squeezed up to the bar, causing some grumbling since Heavy took up enough room for two Americans or three English. They ordered spirits and drank it down and ordered again, because most of the pubs ran out of hard liquor early and had nothing left but warm beer. Nick knew that they could get cold beer at the American Long Bar in the midtown section of Liverpool, but that was a long way from where they were, and he did not want to walk that far for a cold beer.

The barmaid served each of them another warm gin, and they stood against the bar, sipping it silently. As Nick listened to the conversations around them, he thought that it felt good to be on shore with a drink in his hand. There were a few girls at the bar; when they saw Mac and Stringbeans in American merchant marine uniforms, they sidled over to them.

"I say, Yank," one of them said to Mac, "wot's thot costume you're wearing?"

"It ain't a costume," Mac said. "It's a uniform. Ain't you never seen a officer's uniform?"

"Not like thot, I haven't," she said. "Coo."

One of the English merchant seamen moved down the bar and crowded in next to Mac. He was a short, wide man with an ugly pockmarked face and a pot of beer in his hand. He stared contemptuously at Mac. Nick, remembering the battle of Curly's Bar, drank his glass empty and wished he had a pewter mug at hand.

"Bug off, Bertie," the girl said. "You ain't been invited."

"'Tis a free bar," Bertie said truculently. "I'll stand where I please."

"How about moving down about two inches?" Mac asked him politely. "Right now, you're standing on my foot."

"I like it where I am," Bertie said. "'Ow about that, Yank?"

"Get off the gentleman's toot," the barmaid said. She

had a short length of iron pipe in her hand, and looked as if she might be happy to use it. Bertie moved.

"Coo!" Mac's girl said, and laughed. "Ain't he the surly one, now? Standing on a man's slabs o' meat!"

Bertie glowered at her, but did not say anything. The barmaid still had her iron bar in hand, tapping the top of the bar with it gently and suggestively. Nick smiled at her, but she gave him back a blank stare, and he looked away quickly. Apparently she was impartial with her iron bar.

"Give us another round, miss," Heavy said. Heavy did not like fights because he was too slow to run, and offered a large and vulnerable target for an opponent. "Give Bertie one too," he added, smiling at Bertie.

"'Ow about me and Sally 'ere, Yank?" the girl said, giving Mac a gap-toothed smile. "You standing us a drink, Yank?"

"Why not?" Mac said. "Gin?"

"I don't know as I should," she said, reaching for the glass as the barmaid filled it. "Wot I mean, spirits and all, and me not used to it, like."

The smoldering Bertie had a laughing fit that nearly strangled him and earned him dour looks from Sally and her friend. Mac started to say something to him, but Nick kicked him hard on the ankle and he thought better of it. The pub was filled and the bar was four-deep, mostly mercantile navy.

The girl sipped her warm gin politely, with her little finger well out.

"Wot kind of officer are you?" she asked Mac.

"A bloody admiral," Bertie said. "All Yanks are colonels or admirals."

"I'm a mate," Mac told him.

"She is she," Bertie said.

"Here we go again," Nick. "What do you limeys call a deck officer?"

"'Oo you calling a limey, Yank?"

"I'm not *your* mate, love," the girl said to Bertie.

"No offense," Nick said quickly. He saw a small pin on Bertie's coat, and tried to read it. It was about the size of a nickel and it was composed of two letters, "MN."

Bertie turned the pin over so that it read "NW."

"Most of the time, it's Mercantile Navy," he said. "Except when you bloody Yanks are in port, and then we turns it upside down and it stands for No Women."

Stringbeans had been drinking gin as rapidly as he could put them down to get a load on before the barmaid ran out of spirits, so he had paid no attention to the conversation. He was standing next to Mac, and Mac and the two girls were between Stringbeans and Bertie. Unfortunately, above the noise of the crowd, Stringbeans heard Bertie clearly, and laughed.

That was a mistake, Nick thought. He turned to the barmaid and said "A half pint, please," and watched anxiously as she drew the beer. He hoped she would give him the mug before the action started. He looked at Bertie and saw him deliberately finish off his gin and then start purposefully for Stringbeans.

Bertie walked around Mac and punched Stringbeans smartly in the eye. Mac hit Bertie, and a small fat man who had been standing silently behind Nick, listening, hit Nick in the back of the neck. Nick took his beer from the barmaid, drained it, and turned around and hit the small fat man with the mug, which shattered.

"What happened?" Nick asked. "The little fat limey didn't look that tough."

Mac and Stringbeans were supporting him, their hands under his arms.

"We lost," Mac said.

Nick tried to focus his eyes on Mac, but he could not see him in the darkness of the blackout.

"That little limey hit me?" he asked. "He had a hell of a punch if it was him."

"It was the barmaid," Stringbeans told him. "She did it very scientific. Reached over with her little old iron pipe and tapped you on the back of the head like a man driving a tack. Then she hit Bertie a little harder because she must of figured he had a harder head, eh?"

"If he hasn't, he's dead," Nick said, feeling his head again. "She came close to killing me."

"She got Heavy, too," Stringbeans said. "He was sitting on the floor minding his own business, and when he got up, thinking it was all over, she whacked him on the head and knocked him right back down again."

He laughed in the darkness.

"Then he got up with one hand on his head, covering up, and she hit him again, and down he went again."

"Ain't nothing quite as funny as a fractured skull," Heavy said bitterly from somewhere in the dark near Nick. "Unless maybe it's a broken neck."

"You're lucky, love," a woman's voice said. "Sarah was in a happy way tonight. Her old man is back off two years at sea."

"And he's bloody well shipping out again," another voice said. It sounded vaguely familiar to Nick, but it was difficult for him to tell who it was with his ears ringing.

"Arse or 'orse," the girl said, "get your hand off it, love. Whoever you are. That's no way to behave in public."

"Nobody can see," Nick said reasonably, leaving his hand where it was.

The girl did not complain anymore, and moved off slowly into the darkness, with Nick clutching her firmly by the bottom. Behind him, Stringbeans followed with his hand on Nick's shoulder, and Nick guessed that the rest of the party was in single file behind Stringbeans. As they walked through the dark city, he decided, from the sounds of their voices,

that behind Stringbeans came the other girl, Mac, Heavy, and
Bertie.

Nick kept his hand on the flexing and moving rump for
what seemed a long time in the dark and cold, finding it pleasant. The girl in front of him made her way through the blackness as surely as a good navigator.

"When she finally stopped, Nick bumped into her.

"There's a pub here, love," she said. "You can let go
now. Not that I ain't 'ad fun."

They went in through the blackout curtains. The pub
was smaller than the first had been, and not so crowded.

They lined up at the bar, and it was a minute or two
before Nick's eyes adjusted to the brightness after the pure
black of the outside. When he could see clearly again, he discovered that Mac had a mouse under one eye and Stringbeans a fat lip. Bertie had a lump on the back of his head
that, Nick thought, must look something like his own. Sally
had a bump over one eye that gave her face a quizzical cast.

After they ordered gin and were sipping it thankfully,
Nick suddenly realized that they had lost Heavy somewhere
along the way. He pointed this out to the others; they decided
Heavy must have been at the end of the line or there would
have been others missing.

By a process of elimination, they arrived at the conclusion that Bertie had been just in front of Heavy at the end
of the line.

"You remember him letting go of you?" Mac asked
Bertie. The Englishman sipped his gin thoughtfully, and pondered.

"Now that yer mention it," he said slowly, "seems as if
about halfway along he let go. I don't recall if he made fast
again or not, mate."

"We better find him," Stringbeans said. "Me and this
fine lady here will go and look."

"My name is Daisy," the girl said. "Like in the flower of the same name. My friend 'ere is named Sally."

After the introductions were complete, they decided it would be best for all of them to go together to search for Heavy. They lined up at the door and attached themselves to one another like a line of elephants, and Daisy led the way into the dark again.

Luckily, the search was a short one. Within a half block of the pub they heard Heavy complaining.

"I don't know how come we stopped," Heavy was saying. "I'm freezing my ass off, and my head hurts from where someone hit me."

"We're coming," Nick called to him. "Just stand still and keep talking so we can find you."

"I been standing still for half an hour," Heavy said. "Holding on to whoever I'm holding on to."

They moved slowly and carefully through the pitch dark toward Heavy's voice, and Nick, as they drew closer, moved up to the head of the line. He groped with hands outstretched until he felt something soft and warm. He thought he had found Heavy, but he was wrong.

"'Ere, 'ere," a woman's voice said indignantly. "Ain't I been standing 'ere in the grip of a madman for Gord knows 'ow long without being felt all over like a fancy woman by another one?"

"I'm sorry," Nick said. "I thought I had Heavy."

"Don't fash yourself, dearie," Daisy said soothingly from behind him. "It were all a mistake. He got the wrong one by the arse."

"I figured somebody stopped to take a leak," Heavy said. "How come nobody said nothing?"

"I was afraid you would be took violent all of a sudden if I made an outcry," the strange woman said. "'Ow would you like to be going home peaceful-like and all of a sudden have some great lowk of a man clap 'is 'and on you?"

"We're sorry," Nick told her. "Can we buy you a drop of something for your trouble, ma'am?"

"Aye," she said grudgingly. "A drop of spirits might take some of the bite off the cold, now." Nick wanted to light a match to discover what she looked like, but he thought it might not be a very tactful thing to do.

When they got back to the pub, all of them looked at her curiously. She was not too bad for a girl picked up accidentally in the black of night in Liverpool, Nick thought. She was short and fat and she had a blue fly tattooed on one cheek, but she did not look much older than thirty-five. After drinking two quick gins, she accepted Heavy's apologies graciously.

They drank gin until the barmaid ran out of spirits, and then they drank warm beer and ale until she said, "Time, gentlemen!"

By then Heavy had talked the newcomer into submission, which proved to be no great feat. Daisy and Sally had needed even less persuasion to spend the night. Their only problem was where to spend it. They discussed this as they finished their last drinks at the bar.

"It's too cold to do anything outside," Nick said.

"There ain't many vacant rooms to be let in Liverpool," Daisy said unhappily. "And we can't go to my place because me old lady lives with me."

"I know a place," the barmaid said. "But you got to take me along to make the arrangements."

To Nick, she looked no worse than Heavy's girl. They voted to award her to Stringbeans, who grumbled until Nick offered him first choice of fine ladies next time, and Mac pointed out she was better than nothing. Nick told the barmaid it would be all right if she did not mind settling for Stringbeans.

"Any pot in a storm, love," she said to Stringbeans.

She led them through the darkness for a few blocks, then stopped outside a dim doorway. It turned out to be the Young Men's Christian Association dormitory for transient service personnel, and she knew the janitor, a small wisp of a man from Scotland. Nick had to pay him a pound note for his cooperation.

The janitor ushered them into a large and empty dormitory room with double-deck bunks lining the walls. He flashed his light around the room to show them the layout.

"When you do yer business in here, lads," he said, "do it on the bottom bunks. Had a lad in here last week tried to do his business in the top bunk, and the whole thing collapsed. Give him a nasty cut, it did. In a delicate place, if ye ken what I mean."

"I ken," Nick said. "Thanks."

"Where's the head?" Heavy asked.

"Use the fire bucket in the hall," the janitor said. "We've got no rooms wi' bath, lad."

Nick was shivering from the cold by now; the YMCA lacked heat as well as heads, and he waited impatiently for the janitor to leave so that he could climb into one of the bunks and warm up.

When the janitor shuffled out of the room, taking all the light with him when he turned off the flashlight, Nick groped for Sally, found her, and climbed carefully into a lower bunk with her.

Nick had barely embarked upon what the janitor called his business when a tearing crash from across the room brought him out of the bunk, wondering if they had been bombed. The janitor came back in and swept the beam of his flashlight across the room, revealing Heavy and his girl lying naked in the wreckage of a bunk.

Nick was intrigued to discover Heavy's girl friend had

the hindquarters of a fox tattooed on her belly. The front half had disappeared down a crevice.

"'Ave you ever seen the like?" she cried indignantly when the janitor's flashlight revealed her.

"Not in me old age," the janitor said judiciously. "I knew a lass in Glasgow once had a snake much in the same situation, though. But it was in me youth."

"I didn't mean the fox," she said.

"I didn't see more nor the fox and his burrow," the janitor said honestly. "You and your mate better bunk on the floor, lass. There seems to be quite a much of him."

When they awakened in the morning, the girls were gone, and with them most of their money. They had not had much. Nick thought they were lucky to have left the ship too hurriedly to get a draw from the purser, but they still had to walk down to the dock area through the dank, early cold of a Liverpool morning as the fog shredded away from the edges of the gray buildings like dirty smoke.

16

They turned to on deck the next morning, chipping and scraping and red-leading the mast houses and the main deck. The deck cargo had been discharged. The longshoremen were working the hatches, and the deck gang had to paint where they were not working, mostly over the side.

Heavy worked on the top of the mast house just forward of the midship house; Mac and Nick were on the deck of the flying bridge, where they chipped and scraped gently until coffee time. On the mast house, Heavy scraped at a ventilator as delicately as a sunburned bald man scratching his head.

The third mate had turned his watch to checking the

lifeboats, going over them very carefully and making sure they had all provisions required and were seaworthy.

It seemed, to Nick, like almost any day in a foreign port when the first mate required the deck gang to turn to. Not all mates did.

"How far is it to London?" Mac asked him, hitting his section of the deck a very gentle blow with his chipping hammer to loosen the old paint.

"I don't know," Nick said. "I don't remember that I have ever been there. Not too far, I guess."

"Maybe we should go," Mac said. He hit the deck with his hammer in a slow swing beat, and Nick tried an offbeat rhythm around it. It sounded pretty good to Nick.

"If it doesn't take too long," Nick said. Mac put down his chipping hammer and took up a scraper and started to scrape so that it sounded like brushes on a snare drum. Nick fitted his hammer strokes into the new rhythm to imitate the bass and snare drum in a Dixieland combination.

"We can find out," Nick said. He liked the idea of going to London. Liverpool was not exactly the Paris of England.

"You holding?" Mac asked.

"Not after the other night," Nick said. "I'm broke. But we didn't take a draw. Let's check the purser and see how much we can get. Should be two, three hundred bucks, anyway."

"Plus cigarettes," Mac said. "We get a few cartons of cigarettes, they worth more than money."

The bosun came by and stopped to watch them work. They quit talking. Mac put down his scraper and picked up his chipping hammer, and they tapped the deck together, being careful not to hit too hard or too often. They established a good double rhythm, and the bosun listened for some time without comment.

Nick looked up at him once in a while, wondering why

he was watching, but the bosun said nothing. He resembled, Nick thought, a small, fat, featherless owl, his lips sucked in over the toothless gums, and the watery little eyes blinking every time one of the hammers hit the deck.

Finally Mac stopped working and stood up. "What you looking for?" he asked the bosun. "You some kind of company fink?"

"You been working here all morning," the bosun said. "You ain't chipped a square big enough for me to get my ass on. You call that work?"

"We work carefully," Nick said, laying down his hammer and leaning back against a ventilator. He was tired and hung over, and the bosun appeared even more repulsive than usual. "We don't need any toothless old bastard to tell us how to do it."

"He's a fink," Mac said to Nick, ignoring the bosun. "A real company man. The scene about the steaks was just an act. It's ten minutes past coffee time, and he ain't even knocked us off yet."

Nick checked his watch, which showed five minutes after ten. Coffee time was ten o'clock. Mac was nearly right. Union rules specified coffee time at ten in the morning and at three in the afternoon, and it was the bosun's duty to knock off the deck gang at these times.

"Coffee time," Nick said to Mac, and put down his hammer and got up. "You go aft and knock off the guys back there. I'll knock off the crew forward."

"It ain't coffee time until I say it," the bosun said. "You git back to work."

"You want us to bring you up on charges?" Nick asked him sweetly. "You are the guy who had to have the pork chops measured, and now you let us work ten minutes past coffee time. We're taking thirty minutes for coffee, starting now."

"It's an order," the bosun said stubbornly.

"Take your order, and stuff it," Mac told him. He kicked his chipping hammer across the deck. "I'll go aft," he said to Nick.

"Coffee time's only fifteen minutes," the bosun said, spraying Nick with spittle in his excitement.

"You," said Mac slowly and distinctly, "are a toothless old son of a bitch."

"That's what he said," the bosun replied, pointing at Nick.

"I called you a bastard," Nick corrected him.

"You were right," Mac said. "He's both."

"You call me names, and we'll go right to the mate," the bosun said.

Nick went to the forward rail and leaned over and yelled, "Coffee time!" then started down to the messroom. Mac went aft to knock off the deck gang working there, and the bosun followed Nick below.

As they went by the boat deck, Nick made a mental note of it because it was against union rules; he decided to keep track of the time the third and the cadets spent working on deck.

When Nick and the bosun came in, the black gang was already sitting around the tables drinking coffee. The first assistant engineer was sitting with them, drinking his usual straight alcohol in a water tumbler.

"How come you knocked off so late?" Stringbeans asked.

"We got a company fink for a bosun," Nick told him. The bosun was standing directly behind him.

"I ain't no company fink," he said. "A day's work for a day's pay is what I always say."

The first assistant looked at his watch.

"You're a fink," he said. "I knocked off the black gang thirty minutes ago."

"What you doing sitting in the crew's mess?" the bosun said. "You don't belong down here."

"We ast him," Stringbeans said. "Because he ain't a company fink like you, Bosun."

Heavy came in, and the rest of the deck gang followed him. All of them sat down at the tables and waited for the messboy to bring them coffee. Nick could hear the faint tapping sound of the third mate and the deck cadets chipping away on the boat deck overhead, and it made him feel good. Every hour they worked was an hour of overtime for the deck gang. The union rules specified that if anyone but deckhands did deck work, it was overtime for the deck crew.

"The third's a fink," the bosun said uneasily, trying to divert attention from himself. "Hear them deck cadets working up there? He ain't said a word to the first about them doing deck-gang work." He looked at Nick with his little pink eyes. "You the deck delegate," he said. "They doing deck-gang work and stealing our jobs, and you ain't said a word."

"And I'm not about to," Nick said. He drank his coffee and rapped on the cup with his spoon to call the messboy for more.

"Why not?" the bosun asked.

"They can chip and scrape all the overtime hours for us they want," Nick said. "I'm keeping a log on it, and I'll turn it in when we pay off, and we'll collect for every hour they work. I don't mind them working and us getting the money for it."

"He's right," the first assistant said to the bosun. "Teach that snotty little mate a lesson."

"I'm going to say something to the mate," the bosun insisted.

"No, you ain't, Boats," Mac said. "Not and stay healthy, you ain't. That's the deck delegate's business, and Nick is the deck delegate."

"He's supposed to bring up a beef when it happens," the bosun said. He sipped his coffee from a saucer, slurping noisily.

"This isn't a beef," Nick said. "A beef is something you don't like that goes against union rules, like feeding out of two pots."

"Far as I'm concerned," Heavy put in, "I wish he had ten cadets, and could turn 'em to all day so we could get the overtime. It ain't no beef for me, Nick."

"We'll take a vote," Nick said. "All the deck gang is here. All in favor of me keeping a log on the deck cadets' work hours and turning it in for overtime and not taking a beef up to the mate hold up their hands."

All but the bosun held up their hands, even the eight-to-twelve and twelve-to-four watches who were sailing on trip cards and did not have the right to vote.

"All opposed," Nick said. The bosun started to raise his hand, looked around, saw everyone watching him, and pulled it down again.

"Unanimous," Nick announced. "No beef."

The bosun slurped coffee out of his saucer and looked around out of his pink pig's eyes and could think of nothing to say. He looked up at the clock.

"Ten fifteen," he said nastily. "Coffee time is over. All hands on deck."

"We got knocked off late," Mac said. "The delegate said we get thirty minutes' coffee time because you let us go over, and I'm staying here until Nick says coffee time is over."

"I'm the bosun," the bosun said angrily. "And I'm the one turns you to and knocks you off. Not Nick. And I say turn to!"

"I'm the deck delegate," Nick said. "We're not turning to. Go bugger yourself, you toothless old son of a bitch."

"Ever' time I tell you men to do something, someone calls me a toothless old son of a bitch," the bosun said, red

with rage. "I ain't going to stand for it no more. We going
to the mate right now. You come on."

Nobody moved as he stood up and started out of the
messroom. He stopped in the doorway and looked back.

"You hear me?" he said.

"Who you want to go with you?" Mac asked him. "The
whole crew?"

"The delegate," the bosun said. "He's the worst."

"I'll be ready in about twenty minutes," Nick said. "If
you still want me to go to the mate with you when coffee time
is over, I'll go on company time, not on my time."

"The mate's gonna log you," the bosun said. "You
watch."

"And I'm going to log you and bring you up on charges,"
Nick said.

When Nick came out on deck after coffee time, the bosun was waiting for him. They went up to the boat deck to
see the mate, who was watching the third and the two cadets
working.

"What's the matter?" the mate asked. The bosun took
off his cap, and Nick thought for a moment he was going to
tug his forelock as seamen had been wont to do in the days
of wooden ships.

"Sir," the bosun said in a high whine, "this man is
mutinous."

"Mutinous?" the mate asked, looking at Nick quizzically.
The deck cadets quit chipping and looked at the bosun until
the third motioned them to get back to work, and they began
chipping again.

"Ever' time I tell him to do something, he calls me a
toothless old bastard," the bosun said.

"Sometimes's 'son of a bitch,'" Nick said.

"What did you say?" the mate asked Nick, and the
cadets quit chipping again.

"I said I don't always call him a toothless old bastard," Nick told him. "Sometimes I call him a toothless old son of a bitch."

"Why?" asked the mate.

"Because that is what he is," Nick said.

"See?" the bosun interjected eagerly, spraying the mate. "Mutiny."

"That's not mutiny," Nick said to the bosun. "You know the definition of mutiny?"

"No," the mate agreed thoughtfully, "it's not mutiny. Maybe it's insubordination, though."

"It's not that either," Nick said. "After I call him a toothless old bastard, I usually do what he wants me to do."

"It's something," the bosun said vehemently, spraying the first mate again. "It's got to be something."

"Move downwind," the mate said, wiping himself off. "What is it, then?"

"I don't know," the bosun admitted. "You mean it's all right for him to call me that?"

"No," the mate said. "If I give him an order not to and he does, then it *is* insubordination. So don't call him a toothless old anything anymore, Nick. Okay?"

"Aye, aye, sir," Nick said. "I'll think of something else, sir."

"Try to get along," the first said. "We may be on this ship together for a long time."

"How can you get along with a man calls you names?" the bosun whined. "And takes thirty minutes' coffee time. That's another thing I meant to tell you."

"Coffee time is fifteen minutes," the mate told Nick. "I can log you two for one if you go over."

"And it starts at ten and three," Nick said stubbornly. "Boats knocked us off ten minutes late this morning. You put that in the log, too."

"I don't mind if you take twenty minutes," the mate said. "Anyway, I'm not logging you this time, but don't do it again. And don't call the bosun a toothless old son of a bitch no more."

"Aye, aye," Nick said. "Come on, you toothless old offspring of a mangy she-camel."

"See?" the bosun spluttered. "Did you hear that?"

"He said not to call you a toothless old son of a bitch," Nick said reasonably. "I called you a son of a she-camel."

"Don't call him anything but bosun," the first said wearily.

"Fair enough," Nick said. "Come on, Bosun."

The two deck cadets and the third were squatting on their heels, listening and not chipping. The first said to them, "Turn to or I'll call you worse than that."

They started chipping again, and the bosun walked off grumbling to himself, with Nick behind him. They went down to the main deck, where the bosun halted to watch Heavy painting.

He was painting a ventilator on top of the Number Two mast house, working with the care and precision of a Rembrandt. While Nick and the bosun watched unnoticed, Heavy made a careful stroke with his brush and leaned back to eye the result critically.

He contemplated the ventilator silently for a moment, then closed one eye and held up his thumb as if he were measuring a model. Satisfied, he stepped up to the ventilator again and made a little mark with the paintbrush. He had created a rather potbellied woman on the side of the ventilator, and he was so absorbed in giving a lifelike look to her rump that he still did not notice Nick or the bosun.

The bosun and Nick watched in silence for another minute or so while Heavy went through the whole performance again. Nick had to stifle an impulse to applaud.

The bosun moved up closer to the mast house to get

a good look at the picture, and stared at it with his mouth open and his little pink eyes squinting. Then he shook his head as if he could not believe his eyes. He yelled something at Heavy, but the noise of the longshoremen working cargo drowned out his voice, so he picked up a scantling and climbed partway up the ladder leading to the top of the mast house and poked Heavy on the bottom with it.

He did not get a chance to say whatever it was he wanted to say to Heavy because the fat man jumped and kicked his can of gray paint off the mast house onto the bosun. It was nearly a full gallon of paint, since Heavy had used very little on his masterpiece, and the bosun's shout subsided into a gurgle.

The paint can turned over in midair and landed neatly on the bosun's head, and the heavy tide of paint turned him gray from face to knees. The impact knocked him off the ladder and back against the hatch coaming, and he sat suddenly on the edge of the hatch itself, teetering dangerously near to falling down the open hatch.

Nick grabbed him by the arm to keep him from going over, and realized that the deck had grown silent.

Apparently the bosun's anguished howl and gurgle had carried over the noise of the winches. The mate was standing on the wing of the bridge, looking down, and the longshoremen had stopped work.

The bosun seemed dazed at first, and he sat on the edge of the hatch with Nick holding his arm, gazing up at Heavy and dripping gray paint on the deck. Nick was trying not to laugh, but Heavy began to whicker in the start of the high, whooping gasps that served him for laughter, and everyone else began to laugh too, except the bosun.

He spat gray paint and wiped his face, managing only to spread the paint more evenly, then waved to Heavy to come down off the mast house.

It took Heavy a long time to negotiate the descent because he was afraid of ladders, and the eight-foot ladder to
the top of the mast house was narrow and difficult for him.
The bosun kept trying to scrape the paint off as Heavy came
down ponderously and carefully.

When Heavy reached the deck, the bosun eyed him evilly
for a moment, then picked up the paint can and dumped what
paint was left on Heavy, and said. "I'm taking you to the
mate." He grabbed Heavy by the arm and led him aft to the
midship house.

They went up the ladder to the mate on the boat deck,
but before the bosun could say anything the mate made him
move.

"You're dripping where the deck cadets just chipped,"
the first said. "Get over here and drip on the old paint."

The bosun moved over to drip unhappily on the old paint.

"I'm charging this one with malingering and insubordination," he said as formally as he could, under the circumstances.

"'Malingering' means he says he's sick when he isn't,"
the mate said. "He claim to be sick?"

"No," said the bosun. "But he poured paint on me."

"I saw the whole thing," the mate said. "It looked like
an accident to me. You goosed him with a piece of wood.
Might make any man jump."

"Sure as hell made me jump," Heavy said virtuously. "I
didn't know what it was. You can't tell what's sneaking up
behind you after a few weeks at sea."

"He done it on purpose," the bosun insisted.

"I didn't," Heavy rejoined. "You was the only one did
anything on purpose. First you try to bury a scantling in
me; then you poured paint on me. Did you see that part,
Mr. Mate?"

"I saw it," the mate said.

"Sir, I'm just a toothless old man," the bosun said sadly,

wiping at the paint. Nick, who had come up the ladder to see and hear better, thought he sounded like a man who had had his spirit broken.

"I done had more nor a man can bear," the bosun went on. "You seen how he was going about painting that ventilator and all, sir. He was putting a nekkid woman on it."

"It just happened to look that way," Heavy said righteously. "I was just spotting it up where it was rusty."

"Then how come you was holding up your thumb?" the bosun asked.

"I was getting cramps in it," Heavy told him.

"Both of you better get below and clean up," the mate said. "That paint is drying on you, and you're making a puddle on the deck."

"You ain't gonna log him?" the bosun asked wistfully. "Maybe a day's pay?"

"No," the mate said shortly. "Get below."

The bosun turned away wearily and went below. Heavy waited for a moment and went after him. Nick followed the two of them and helped Heavy get the paint off with paint remover, which took a liberal amount of skin as well. The bosun worked on himself alone, and was not very successful.

When he appeared in the messroom for supper, he was still a dirty battleship gray. It was, Nick thought, an improvement on his usual color, which was just dirty.

"Looks pretty good on you," he said to the bosun, but the old man did not answer him. Nick felt sure that his spirit was broken, but he was wrong. The old man was just brooding.

17

The *Andrew Crichton* lay at dockside on the Clyde in Liverpool harbor for six more days, discharging cargo, then moved to another dock to take on ballast for the trip home.

Nick worked with the rest of the deck gang during the day, and they got most of the deck and the mast houses scraped and red-leaded and painted. The bosun stayed out of the way, other than to open the paint locker in the morning and lock it after the paint had been stowed away for the night.

Heavy was assigned by the mate to paint the hatch coamings, which meant he did not work much, since he could paint only when the longshoremen were not working cargo. The hatch coamings did not inspire his artistic yearnings.

The *Crichton* took on ballast at a small port called Swansea; then the crew turned to to batten down and secure for sea. It was early, gray morning when they steamed out to make their convoy rendezvous.

Nick was at the wheel as the Liberty moved out into open water, and he found her more difficult to steer, riding high in the water with only ballast in the holds. The high sides acted like sails in the wind, but fortunately there was only a light breeze as they stood out to sea, and the *Crichton* answered the wheel well enough.

The convoy made up on a cloudy, cold morning with the sea just beginning to kick up so that now and then Nick could see a small flash of white across the broad rolling steeliness of the water when an especially big wave broke. The *Crichton* was again the lead ship in its column; the newer, presumably faster ships were placed first so that they would not run up on the slower vessels.

As usual, it took a good part of the day to get the convoy squared away with every ship in place. The corvettes of the escort skittered back and forth through the big merchant ships like dogs nipping at the heels of big gray cows, herding them into position, yapping at the slower ones with the quick flash of blinker lights.

"In about three weeks we'll be on Bourbon Street, drinking whiskey and chasing B girls," the first mate said to Nick as they stood on the wing of the bridge watching the other ships slowly working themselves into position. "It's gonna feel good."

Nick had forgotten about his problem with Rusty, but the mate's words brought it back to his mind, and he shook his head gloomily.

"I got a B girl who is going to be chasing me," he said sadly. "Her and her two brothers and a lawyer."

"You get her in trouble?" the mate asked, and Nick nodded.

"Don't worry about it," the first said philosophically. "I been in the same boat a few times. I figure if you stay away three months or more, it's all over one way or another by the time you get back."

"How so?" Nick asked. "Looks to me like it's going to be worse. She'll be showing by the time we get to New Orleans."

"The B girls always got two or three merchant marines they can blame it on," the mate said. "Since you ain't there, she's gonna get one of the other ones. You wait and see."

"Not much else I can do," Nick said. "Maybe we won't pay off in New Orleans, anyway."

"Probably will, though," the mate said, unhelpfully. "This is a Waterman ship, and New Orleans is home port for her."

The *Andrew Crichton* was making slow headway, chugging placidly through the sea, waiting for the convoy to shape up. As lead ship, the *Crichton* had taken station early, lining up with the lead ships on each beam, then waiting for the rest of the column to fall in behind.

The convoy commodore was in a big tanker a couple of columns away; the blinker on the tanker was going almost constantly as he sent instructions to the merchant ships and the escorts. Once it blinked rapidly at the *Crichton,* and the mate cursed under his breath and looked up at the stack.

"We're making smoke," he said, and started into the wheelhouse to call the engine room. Captain Haraldsen was already at the speaking tube, and Nick could hear the tall, lean old man yelling from the wing of the bridge. The smoke thinned and died away.

It was late in the day when, at last, all the ships were in position, and the convoy steamed off into the North Atlantic, a big square of gray merchant ships riding high in ballast, six miles across and six deep, moving at a steady eight knots. The skies had cleared, and night came cold and bright with a full moon silvering the broad, heavy-looking swells.

"Submarine moon," Mac said to Nick as they stood on the main deck for a few minutes before going in to the messroom.

"That's right," Nick said uneasily. The black silhouettes of the other ships in the convoy stood out clearly against the sheen of the sea and the light of the moon. "Makes you feel like a sitting duck in a shooting gallery."

"We're still too close in," Mac said cheerfully. "They ain't gonna come in this close after us."

"You hope," Nick said.

"I hope," Mac agreed. "Come on, Nick, let's eat. Then I'm gonna be ready for some sack time. We like to wore ourselves out last night with them fine ladies."

"I'm ready," Nick said. He had not slept at all the night before in Swansea. All the crew not on watch had spent the last night ashore.

They ate quickly and went to bed, and Nick lay tossing for a few moments, thinking about the submarine moon, but there were no alarms during his watch, below, and when the twelve-to-four ordinary called him for the morning watch, the ship was moving smoothly through the gentle swells, lifting to them easily, the rigging creaking only a little and the steady thump of the engine already as familiar to Nick as his heartbeat.

The *Crichton* was riding smoothly enough, but she was rolling a good deal. Riding as high in the water as she did in ballast, it took only small seas to make her wallow, and Heavy was having his usual trouble with his belly. Nick climbed down from the top bunk and grinned at the fat man as he started getting dressed. Mac was sitting on the other lower bunk, pulling on his shoes.

"We might try making a sling for it," Mac said cheerfully. "Maybe we could rig it from the overhead so Heavy could lie on his side and put his belly in it, kind of like in a hammock."

"Don't do me no favors," Heavy said. "Anyway, I don't sleep on my side."

"If he would sleep on his belly, we could shore him up fore and aft with pillows," Nick said. "We could probably get the steward to give us some extras for a good cause."

"I don't know," Mac said doubtfully. "It would take maybe four pillows, two under his chin and two under his knees."

Heavy gave them explicit directions on how to dispose of their pillows, and they left, stopping at the head on their way to the messroom. They drank their coffee quickly, and Nick went to take the first wheel watch. While he had been sleeping, heavy black clouds had covered the moon, and he was glad to find the night black and impenetrable.

"Looks like heavy weather coming up," the AB on watch said when Nick took the wheel from him. He gave Nick the course, and Nick repeated it.

"She don't steer so good light," the AB said. "If you don't watch her, she can veer ten points in a squall."

"I'll watch her," Nick told him. "When did the weather turn dirty?"

"When we came on watch," the AB said. "About midnight, maybe a little later. I like it better clear."

"You won't like it when you have been going to sea a while," Nick said dryly. "You like to be a target?"

"I never thought of that," the AB said, and went below.

The first mate came into the wheelhouse, yawning and sleepy, and the captain came in after him. The second mate talked to them for a few moments, and left the bridge.

At the wheel, Nick experimented gently with the response of the *Crichton*, trying to judge how she was reacting. He could not establish a pattern; the shifting, squally winds made the ship as skittish as a colt.

"Quiet night," the first said to Captain Haraldsen. Nick could barely make them out, standing side by side at the front of the wheelhouse, near the ports, looking out at the black night.

"Aye," the captain said. "Too quiet, Mr. Mate. The last three trips we have made have been too quiet. I don't like it."

"Barometer's falling," the first said. "Should be rough by first light."

"Aye," the captain said. He was quiet as he looked out, a tall, thin, deeper blackness in the dark of the room. "How is she answering, Quartermaster?" he asked Nick over his shoulder.

"Skittery, sir," Nick said. "Feels like she may be too high by the stern. No bite to the rudder."

"We should have taken on more ballast," the captain said to the first. "I wish we had had more time."

"Maybe we could flood the stern tanks," the first said. "Might give her a better trim."

"We'll leave her as she is," the captain said. "She'll be all right. She may wander a bit but she'll come back quick enough."

"Aye, aye, sir," the first said, and Nick gave his attention to the compass needle.

The needle crept away from the course, and Nick put on wheel slowly to bring it back. He used almost a full turn, and had to leave half of it on when he steadied her.

"She's taking nearly a turn of wheel," he said to the first.

"Aye," the first said. "Wind's freshening and steadying on the port bow. Tell me if she needs more."

"It's a good thing we had the hydraulic cylinder fixed, mister," the captain said. "We'd be in a hell of a fix if the same thing happened to us here that happened off Hatteras. If we missed all the ships in the convoy, we'd still be a laggard with no escort."

The weather grew steadily worse during Nick's wheel watch, and he was happy to relinquish the wheel to Mac when it was over. He had a quick cup of coffee and fought his way forward along the pitching deck to take his trick on lookout.

He found the fat man crouched miserably under the forward guntub. As Nick reached him, a heavy sea smashed into the bow, spraying them with water, and Heavy cursed.

"Stand by on the port wing of the bridge," Nick yelled in Heavy's ear, over the howling of the freshening wind. "The old man's afraid this wind may carry a ship from the next column into us."

Heavy yelled something back that Nick did not understand, then stumbled off down the deck. Nick braced himself in the bow and stared into the darkness, trying to see ahead.

The cold bit through his oilskins and the two sweaters and long underwear, and Nick settled himself grimly for the long vigil. If it got worse, the old man would have to set lookouts up on the bridge.

Halfway through his watch, Nick opened the forepeak hatch and went below out of the wind long enough to let his face mask thaw so that he could free it where it had frozen to his lips. When he had pulled it loose, he went back up into the bow.

It seemed a long time before Mac came up to relieve him in the first dim grayness of dawn.

"Heavy is on the wheel," he yelled to Mac. "The first says for you to take ten, then relieve him. He can't hold her in this weather."

18

As Nick struggled aft, he met the crews for the forward guntubs coming up to stand by for general quarters. They moved in short rushes along the deck, waiting for the ship to recover from her heavy rolls, and for the green water to sluice off the deck. The wind was still building.

Over the side the seas raced by, heavy and high, and Nick thought the wind must have reached gale force by now. The noise on deck was deafening with the steady crash and slam of the seas and the whoop of the wind in the steel rigging and the metallic clash and bang of gear slamming on the deck or against steel bulkheads.

The warmth of the messroom was pure pleasure. Nick

helped himself to a half cup of coffee and braced himself in a chair while he drank it in quick sips when the ship paused and shuddered between rolls.

He had not finished when the saloon messboy came in and said: "The first wants you on the wheel right now. Says for me to bring your coffee up there. How you want it?"

"Black and hot," Nick said.

He went up to the wheelhouse, where he found the first at the wheel with Heavy watching him. The captain was standing with legs wide apart, rolling with the ship's movement, staring out at the gray and tumultuous seas.

"You can't wait," the first was explaining to Heavy. "You got to meet her before she starts swinging too fast, else she winds up in the trough, and you'll never get her back. See?"

"I guess so," Heavy said sourly.

"I'll take it," Nick said to the first.

The first gave him the wheel, and Nick set himself to hold the course against the wind and the weather. The compass needle swung wildly back and forth, and Nick had to balance the swings on each side of the course to estimate if he were on the heading or not.

"Get some coffee and then stand lookout on the wing," the first said to Heavy, who nodded and lumbered away.

"She's taking nearly two full turns of left wheel," the first said to Nick. "The cylinder's all right. It's just the wind and the high seas."

"We have a course change coming up before long," the captain said. "That should ease her considerably."

"We flooded the tanks," the first told Nick. "She steers a little better, but she's still nervous. You'll have to look lively. If she gets in the trough in these seas, light in ballast as she is, she could roll over."

"Aye, aye, sir," Nick said seriously. He eased on another half-turn of left wheel when the mate went to talk to the old man. If the *Andrew Crichton* rolled over in this sea and this weather, the rescue ships of the convoy would pick up nothing but quick-frozen merchant seamen, if they could find them.

Nick was well aware of the dangers of the North Atlantic in winter. Once he had gone to visit a former shipmate in hospital who had been in the water for a few minutes before he was picked up. He had lost both hands and feet to the icy water. Nick decided he would put on his survival suit when he went below. It offered a small additional margin of time in icy water.

Although Nick was exhausted from the physical effort and the intense concentration of a full watch of walking a tightrope with a ten-thousand-ton ship, he got no rest when the eight-to-twelve took over. He repaired to the messroom and ate a meal of scrambled eggs that the chief cook, by some miracle, had managed to produce, then went to the fo'c's'le and put on his survival and turned to with the rest of the watch below, rigging lifelines along the main deck so that the navy gun crews could reach their guntubs in relative safety. It was hard, cold, dangerous work.

Even as high as the *Andrew Crichton* rode in the water, she was taking green seas over the side, and the deck gang worked between floods that swept the deck, holding on to whatever they could find when the water came thick and heavy over the rail. It took the whole morning to finish a job that could have been done in fifteen minutes in normal weather.

By the time they knocked off and straggled into the messroom for lunch, the cook had given up trying to prepare warm meals, and served them cold cuts. The clanging of pots and pans tumbling back and forth in the galley made it clear that they were lucky to get anything. The Liberty seemed to have settled into a regular rhythm of rock and roll. Nick thought that if the weather held without worsening, she would survive.

He slept for three hours in his survival suit, so tired that not even the gyrations of the tortured ship could keep him awake. When the watch was called, he was dismayed to find that the weather had reached new fury.

Standing the first lookout on the wing of the bridge, Nick had to hang onto the rail with both hands and brace himself against the thrust of the wind. He looked back at the convoy in the odd orange light of the day and saw it beginning to lose its precise oblong pattern. A Liberty two columns away and astern of the *Crichton* was dropping back slowly, black smoke pouring from her stack, and a C-2 behind was changing course to avoid her. The lines were growing ragged, even in daylight. Nick wondered what would happen when night came and the ships could not keep station visually.

The first mate came out of the wheelhouse and stood by Nick, holding the rail and balancing surely against the lift, turn, drop, turn, lift of the ship's movement. They were on the bridge deck two levels above the main deck, but when the *Crichton* rolled, the heavy, glassy-looking waves hurtled by almost level with them.

The spray from the waves and the occasional squalls ripped across the deck like bird shot, blown flat and hard by the wind.

The mate yelled something, but Nick could not hear him. The ship rolled hard to port, and Nick and the mate hung from the rail, looking up at the low gray clouds scudding by. She hung for a long time, and Nick could feel himself pulling hard against the rail, as if he could right her by main force. He looked down the long slant of her side to the orange underbelly showing below. Then there was a shocking crash from the other side of the *Crichton*, and she seemed almost to sigh as she began to come back slowly.

As she recovered, the first went across the slant of the deck in a scrambling rush, with Nick close behind him. By the time they were in the wheelhouse, the ship had rolled far to starboard, and they had to fight their way up the steep hill of the deck to reach the door to the port wing.

The first looked forward, then moved aft and looked down on the boat deck, and pointed. This was the weather side of the ship, and the wind, not broken by the bulk of the midship house, poured against Nick with the solid mass of a deep, fast river.

Nick lifted his arm to protect the side of his face from the stinging spray, and looked down at the boat deck. The monstrous wave that had jarred the ship had come up over the boat deck and smashed against the side of the midship house. One of the lifeboats on the boat deck had been carried away, davits and all, with only raw scars in the steel to show where it had been.

The other boat was upside down in its chocks, the heavy steel davits with their long worm screws bent and twisted. The hull of the boat was smashed in as though it had been hit by a gigantic sledgehammer. The movement of the ship was slamming the boat back and forth violently, and the bent davits were about to tear loose.

The first tugged at Nick's arm, and motioned. Nick followed him into the wheelhouse, out of the wind and the noise and the cold.

"Call the watch below," the first said. "We'll have to secure that boat before she tears loose and does more damage."

Nick went below and called the watches and the bosun, and came back to the wheelhouse. The first was talking to the captain about changing course so that the ship would be heading into the seas instead of taking them on the port bow, where they would interfere with the work on the boat deck.

"We can't do that," the captain said. "We can't change course in convoy."

"That means we got to work on the weather deck, then," the mate said grimly. "We got the wind at us there, and we got the chance of another sea like the last one coming aboard."

"I can't change course," the captain said. "Rig safety lines and do the best you can."

"Come on," the first said, and Nick followed him out into the storm.

They rigged lines along the bulkhead first, securing them to the rail there, working on the starboard roll of the ship and clinging to the rail when she came back to port. Luckily, the *Crichton* did not take any green water over the boat deck while they worked, although the seas were breaking green over the main deck. The ship wallowed and strained and labored, but she stayed steadily on course.

One of the skid rails had broken loose and was hammering the side of the ship, smashing into the rail of the passageway alongside the midship house on the main deck. The skid rail was a heavy length of steel girder designed to bridge the open space between the main deck and the boat deck.

The skid rails made it possible to lower away a lifeboat down the high side of a listing ship; for without the rails, the lifeboats would jam in the open space between the main deck rail and the bottom of the boat deck.

At the moment, the loose skid rail was not doing much damage, other than battering in the main deck rail, but the thunderous smash at irregular intervals as it hit the rail seemed to Nick to be the very sound of disaster.

When the safety lines had been rigged, the first motioned for the deck gang to follow him, and they went into the saloon mess to rest and to listen to the mate explain how they would secure the lifeboat. Nick borrowed a cigarette from the saloon messboy, and took a deep drag. The bosun had assembled U-bolts, block and tackle, steel cable, and line. The first checked over the equipment, then explained.

"We'll have to stay out there for quite a while," he said calmly. "I want every man to secure himself to the safety line with a line long enough to reach the lifeboat. But try to get back to the bulkhead and hang on to the rail when she rolls to port."

He told them where he wanted them to make fast to the lifeboat and where to anchor the securing lines to the rail and to the U-bolts set in the deck. After they had finished their cigarettes, he said, "Let's go," and they went back out into the maelstrom.

There were eleven men working on the narrow deck, working in a wind loaded with small knives of icy spray that cut Nick's face until it bled. His hands grew so cold that he had no feeling in them.

It took them an hour to get a heavy line secured to the forward ringbolt of the lifeboat and led back to the rail along the bulkhead, then hauled tight with the block and tackle.

In the hour, two more waves broke over the boat deck and sprawled men helter-skelter. They clung to the rail or to the tackle as the water tore at them, and once Nick found himself clinging to one of the davits, hoping desperately that the sea would not carry it away and him with it.

During the second hour on the boat deck, as they fought to secure the stern of the boat, Nick could see only through a pink blur, and he could not feel the line he tried to bend to the after ringbolt. The rope had begun to ice. It was stiff and hard to manipulate, and Nick worked with one arm around the twisted after davit, sometimes with the first holding him around the waist to steady him. His eyes were slitted against the cutting icy spray, and it took him nearly half an hour to tie a bowline through the ringbolt. He could have tied it in ten seconds in good weather.

The waves soaked him, and the cold made him slow and tired; he lost track of time, and fought with the wind and the sea and the stubborn rope blindly and unthinkingly. He finally got the bowline tied, and waited dully for the ship to roll away from the seas so close below him; then he scrambled back to the bulkhead, and clung to the rail welded there. He turned his face away from the wind and squeezed his eyes shut, trying to clear them of salt and tears.

When he looked back at the lifeboat, he saw that the line he had just secured was fouled on a ragged remnant of a davit from the lifeboat that had carried away. It would be impossible to haul the line light without severing it.

Nick saw what had happened through a pink haze, and cursed stupidly. He was not sure he could muster courage to go back and do it over again, and none of the AB's had enough sea time. He had just about forced himself to let go of the rail when he saw the old bosun scuttle quickly across the deck, now sloping again toward the sea.

His sou'wester had blown away, and the bald head was fringed with ice frozen to the scant hair over his ears. The ship was rolling far to port, and Nick thought for a moment the sea would climb over the boat deck, but the bosun ignored it, scrambling crab-fashion toward the fouled line. He reached it safely and hung on grimly until the ship started back, loosening the line, then he calmly flipped the line free. It was cool and daring seamanship, and Nick felt a surge of admiration for the old man.

When the ship came back, the lifeboat shifted and settled gently against the bosun's leg. The bosun tried to clear himself, but could not. Nick let go and skidded across the deck to his side. He braced himself against the side of the boat, and shoved; it moved, and the bosun was free again. The two of them scrambled together back to the bulkhead, the bosun dragging his injured leg and leaning on Nick.

They hauled the second line taut, snugging the lifeboat as securely as possible against its chocks, and the mate motioned to them to leave the deck.

They snapped free their safety lines and made it into the midship house on the next favorable roll. They followed the first into the saloon mess and collapsed into chairs and sat dripping blood and water for a long time before anyone said or did anything.

Then the mate went over to the bosun and rolled up his trouser leg and looked at his shin and felt it.

"It's cut and bruised, but I don't think it's broken, Boats," he said. "How does it feel?"

"Good enough," the bosun told him. He looked at the mate through tired rheumy eyes, even pinker now from the spray. A thin trickle of blood ran down his leg, but the bosun grinned his toothless grin.

"I can run the deck gang sitting on my ass," he said defiantly.

They went below then, and Nick was surprised to find that during their labors his watch had passed. Mac had spent the whole four hours on the wheel and Heavy on lookout.

Nick was too tired to eat. He took off the wet, icy clothes he had worked in, and climbed into his bunk. As he drifted off to sleep, he thought about the bosun, and smiled. Boats had done a hell of a thing.

Some time while Nick slept, the *Crichton* took another big sea over the boat deck. It carried away the lifeboat and the davits and the rail to which they had been secured.

19

The wind began to die and the waves to flatten out during the next day, and the sky turned a light milky blue. Later it was a deep clear blue, and by the time night came again, the North Atlantic had subsided into big, slow swells as a last reminder of the storm that had passed.

At the end of the evening watch, the moon came up three-quarters full, and Nick could again see the dark shapes of the convoy ships outlined on the bright shield of the sea, most of them in position again, moving silently through the gleaming night like a herd of elephants performing a solemn march.

The convoy was three days out of Liverpool. Nick found

out from the mate that the gale had sunk two corvettes and an old Liberty, which had broken in two. The mate had heard about the losses via blinker from the commodore just before dusk. Nick found he felt no strong emotion. The blinker seemed impersonal, and there was nothing it could say about how it felt to be suddenly cast into the waters of the North Atlantic in winter.

A life raft forward on the port side had carried away during the night, and the loss of two lifeboats and the raft left the *Crichton* short of craft to take off the crew if the ship should be torpedoed.

"It doesn't make much difference," Nick said to the first. "The two times I got it, the shock of the torpedo hitting buggered up the worm gears on the lifeboat davits, and we couldn't lower them away. Best thing to do is kick loose a raft and jump over the side after it."

"That wouldn't help here," the mate told him. "In this water you'd freeze your balls off before you could swim to the raft and climb on it."

After Nick was relieved on the wheel watch, he went out on the boat deck where the crew had worked the day before. The debris had been cleared away, and the deck looked curiously bare with no davits and no boats and only the torn places in the steel deck to show where they had been. The only wind now came from the headway of the *Crichton*. The sea moved in long, diminishing swells, and the ship moved through it easily and quietly.

Nick watched Heavy walking forward to take his post as lookout, a big dark mass in the moonlight. The bright light dimmed briefly as a high thin scurf of cloud slipped across the face of the moon. It was bright again as Nick went below for a quick coffee before standing his watch on standby.

The mate came out and stood with him on the wing for a while after he had returned. Mac was on the wheel, and the convoy pounded along steadily, the wake of the *Crichton* stretching straight and clean across the black of the sea.

"Where is the old man?" Nick asked.

"Sleeping, I guess," the mate said. "Been up thirty-six hours without sleep. He's too old for much of that."

"The wheel is easy now," Nick said. "Half-turn either way keeps her steady as she goes."

"You want some coffee?" the mate asked, and Nick nodded.

"I'll get it," Nick said.

"I got to go to the chart room anyway," the mate answered. "I'll bring it."

He came back in a few minutes, and Nick was grateful for the warmth of the coffee.

"Thanks," he said. "Funny how just one cup of hot coffee can keep you warm a long time." They drank together in silence.

"You been down on the main deck?" the mate asked. "Kind of tore up in places. Lucky we didn't have deck cargo. We would have lost it."

"I guess so," Nick said. "I'm glad it's quiet now, anyway."

"Not too long ago, I would rather have had the storm," the mate said.

"Me too," Nick replied. "When we were catching hell from the subs."

"I was sailing second then," the first said. "We were carrying a load of bombs from New York to Liverpool. We had been discharging about five days, and I went into the American Bar there and ran into some air-force guys. It was early on a night about as bright as this one."

He drank more of his coffee and looked out at the shining sea.

"They asked me what I did, and I told them," he said.

"Then they asked me what kind of cargo I brought over, and I told them that, too."

Ahead, Nick could see the circling shape of a destroyer. He watched it moving across the shine of the sea.

" 'Bombs for you guys to deliver,' I told them," the first said. "Then they said they was flying a mission in the early morning, and asked me if I wanted to deliver them the rest of the way. 'It'll be a good time for it,' one guy told me. 'It's a bomber's moon tonight, and we'll find the target easy.' "

The first was silent for a few moments, and he and Nick watched the black water slip silently by off the port beam.

"Did you go?" Nick asked.

"I told him no, thanks," the first said. "I thought about the people under the bombs looking up at that bright moon and knowing they was going to get it, and I knew just how they felt. I been under bomber's moons in the Med, and a bomber's moon is a torpedo moon, too. The subs can find us tonight if they are out there looking."

Nick shivered slightly and drank the rest of his coffee. It seemed a long time after that before he went off watch, but the watch itself was quiet enough. Dawn came and turned into daylight, and the gun crews went to general quarters and came back. Nick slept heavily during most of the daylight hours on his watch below. Nothing happened, and by the time he was called and had had his coffee and put on his heavy gear again, he had forgotten his fears. The convoy moved serenely and safely over the quiet surface of the sea.

Out along its edges, ahead of the *Andrew Crichton,* the corvettes and destroyers switched back and forth nervously, like sheep dogs with the smell of wolf in their nostrils. Once in a while Nick saw a destroyer squat and start to throw a high bow wave, white against the gray of the dusk as she reached flank speed, and he would hear, faintly, the *Whoop, whoop, whoop!* of her siren.

The destroyers did not lay any eggs. Nick thought maybe the subs had been whipped at last, and he reached the point where he did not worry when he saw a corvette or a destroyer take off on a simulated depth-charge run.

Full dusk came while Nick was on standby. The captain no longer wanted two lookouts now; he let the standby stay in the messroom, warming himself and drinking coffee.

It was just before time for the blackout, and Nick was standing by a porthole, waiting for his coffee to cool and watching a Liberty in the next column riding easily over the nearly calm sea. She had the slow, rocking motion of a cantering horse, lifting her bow easily, holding it for a moment, then dropping it as the swell moved aft to pick up her stern. It was a graceful thing, and Nick enjoyed watching it.

Then her bow and stern lifted at the same time.

They bent across the top of a swell, and she broke in two just forward of the midship house. The bow pointed up at the darkening sky and slipped under the water; the stern raised its screw into the gently graying dusk, then rolled over, and Nick could see tiny black specks that were men sliding down the rusty orange side and over the bottom. The stern floated for a minute and sank, and only an empty sea showed where the ship had been.

It was too far and too dark now for Nick to see the men in the water. There could not have been many survivors.

It was quiet in the messroom. Nick looked away from the porthole, gripped by a sense of unreality. The messboy and an AB from the eight-to-twelve were drinking coffee and reading.

He started to say something to them, and then he felt and heard the *thump, thump, thump* of depth charges exploding in the sea, the concussion ringing against the hull of the Liberty with the muffled sound of a great bell rung by a padded clapper.

Nick put his coffee down and started to run for the deck as the general alarm went off, seven short rings of the alarm bell. The gun crew, which had begun to turn out for general quarters, raced for the guntubs; and the watch below came out on deck, pulling on their gear as they ran.

Nick reached the bridge deck with the gun crews for the 20-millimeters on the wings of the bridge, and went into the wheelhouse to stand by for orders from the captain or the mate. Mac was on the wheel, and Heavy was on lookout. Fleetingly, Nick was sorry for Stringbeans, down in the bowels of the ship in the engine room.

Darkness was coming quickly now, and the first motioned for Nick to take lookout on the wing. Nick went out and stood staring back at the ships of the convoy, and as he looked, a tanker two columns away and astern of the *Crichton* flared suddenly in a blossoming red explosion, and began to burn. Nick had time to notice the path of red the flame laid across the water before he heard the heavy *Blam* of the explosion and felt the shock jar the ship.

He looked away from the burning tanker. Ahead of his ship, he could barely see a destroyer in the fading light, with two corvettes. They were a mile or so away, circling. As he watched, the escorts, dim against the night sky, sank low at the stern and accelerated, and he could make out the slow tumbling shapes of depth charges flung up and out by their Y-guns. The destroyer's bow lifted as her speed built up.

"I hope they got something," the first said, next to him.

He was looking back at the fading glow of the burning tanker, and shook his head. "Poor bastards," he said. Nick did not have to ask him what he meant because he knew that if there were men in the water from the ships that had been torpedoed, the concussion of the exploding depth charges could kill them.

Nick felt the quick succession of hammer blows against

the hull of the Liberty as the depth charges exploded one after another. He strained his eyes into the growing darkness ahead, but he could not see anything.

Another ship in the convoy fired a flare, and the captain, who had come out on deck from the wheelhouse, cursed. In the light of the flare, Nick could see the destroyer and the two corvettes again, closer, and the destroyer suddenly opened fire with its deck guns.

The young ensign in charge of the gun crew said. "They must have brought one up, but I can't see anything."

"There it is," the first said. Nick stared ahead, but all he could see was the bright orange flash of the destroyer's deck guns. Then, low on the water, he saw an answering flash, and in its brief glow the low, oblong outline of the superstructure of a submarine. He felt an intense excitement now, and an imperative need to do something, but there was nothing for him to do. He stood tensely, watching.

The forward gun on the *Crichton* fired unexpectedly, and the flash nearly blinded Nick. The gunnery officer grabbed the intercom to the gun stations and yelled, "Don't fire! Cease fire!" but even as he yelled, the big gun fired again.

Nick opened his mouth against the blast of the firing, and realized, dimly, that the 20-millimeters had started firing, too. He looked ahead again, and as he did so, there was a blinding flash of blue flame from where he had last seen the destroyer and the submarine, and with startling suddenness, the night was quiet.

The shattering noise of the explosion came almost at once. It must have been close, Nick thought.

"That was the destroyer," the mate said. "She must have took a fish. Jesus!"

The *Crichton* steamed steadily on toward the explosion, and Nick said: "I hope to God somebody got the submarine, too. We're headed right for it."

"You better go up in the bow," the first said. "See if you can make out anything from there."

It was very dark and quiet, and as Nick made his way forward as rapidly as he could, he heard, faintly, a sound like the mewing of kittens. He wondered if someone on board had smuggled a cat on board in England.

As he reached the bow, one of the gunners in the tub over his head called out, "Red light bearing one point off the starboard, and closing!" Nick searched the black surface of the sea until finally he saw the faint pinprick of red. He could smell the burned powder from the big gun, and the mewing was growing louder. He saw two more pricks of red light bearing dead ahead, and he yelled back to the bridge, "Two red lights down low bearing straight ahead!"

"Stand by on deck to cast off a raft!" the mate bellowed, and Nick realized that the faint lights were on the life jackets of men in the water. The mewing, very close now, was the sound of their cries for help. They were not calling loudly and they did not use words. It was an inarticulate, crying sound that made Nick sick.

All that he could see of the men in the sea as the *Crichton* swept by was the red lights. There were two men in the water on the port side, and one to starboard so close that for a moment Nick thought the ship would run him down.

But the tiny red light lifted and dipped from the swell of the bow wave, and then slipped quickly astern and the voices wailing in the cold dark died away. As they went by, the bosun tripped a life raft and it went into the sea with a rushing clatter and a splash, and Nick ran back along the rail and watched to see if the red lights in the water would move toward it, but he lost them before he could tell.

For a moment, Nick felt the stabbing guilt of a survivor in combat, a feeling that in some way the men in the water were his fault. He knew the *Crichton* could not stop to pick them up. There was another ship in the darkness dead astern, and the captain could not risk the lives of a full crew for three burned men in the water.

They stayed at general quarters for another hour, but the sea was quiet and there were no more explosions in the night. The gun crews secured and walked aft, talking excitedly, and an AB from the eight-to-twelve came forward to relieve Nick.

Nick walked back along the black deck, shivering. It was not fear. It was an aching deep sadness and a rending sense of futility.

20

On the morning watch, four more merchant ships were sunk. This time the attack came on the far edge of the convoy, and all Nick saw of it was the flash when a ship was hit.

He felt the faint thumping of depth charges as the escort struck back at the submarines, but the danger seemed remote. He stood a two-hour wheel watch because the captain had taken Heavy off the wheel for the duration of the emergency. Nick and Mac split the wheel time.

The crew went on double watches, four hours on and four off. The gun crews were at general quarters all the daylight hours, but the attack lasted only during the gray of dawn.

"You ever see attacks like this?" Nick asked the mate near the end of his stint on the wheel.

"Not me," the first replied. "They must be trying something new. There must be a lot of subs out there."

"I hope they're through with us," Nick said.

"I wouldn't bet on it," the mate replied. "Tell your watch to wear their survival suits on and off watch from now on."

"Okay," Nick said. "I hope we won't need them."

When he went off watch, he went down to the messroom for his breakfast. It was bright day now, and he decided he could wait until after he had eaten before putting on the bulky and uncomfortable survival suit. The messroom was crowded; the watches below from the engine room and the deck gang were all there. None of them felt like sleeping.

Nick was surprised to discover that he was ravenously hungry until he remembered that he had not eaten at all the night before. He was eating a double helping of scrambled eggs and pancakes when the music on the ship's radio, piped into the messroom, stopped, and an English voice said, "We are suspending this program on the BBC to bring you an important message from the Prime Minister. Mr. Winston Churchill."

The conversation stopped.

The familiar voice of Winston Churchill came on, and Nick listened carefully.

"For almost a year," Churchill said, "we have had no appreciable losses to submarines in the Battle of the North Atlantic." The seamen looked at one another. Heavy started to say something, but Nick held up his hand for quiet. "Now one of our convoys on the North Atlantic is under attack," Churchill went on. "As I speak to you the convoy is fighting off an attack by a wolf pack we estimate to be made up of from fifteen to thirty submarines."

He went on, but what he had to say was drowned out in the sudden babble of talk in the messroom. This was the first time any of the crew had ever heard of a wolf pack. It seemed much worse than the attacks Nick had undergone before, carried out by two or three subs at the most.

The talk died down in a few moments, and Nick could hear Churchill again. He was nearing the end of his brief talk.

"So," he was saying, "the Battle of the North Atlantic, which we had begun to hope well won, is joined again. To win it, we will need all the courage and all of the strength of the brave men who man the merchant fleets of the free countries. God help them."

There was a long silence when he had finished, and then the music started again. Nick finished his coffee and stood up, thinking of the wolf pack.

"We'd better put on the survival suits," he said to Mac. "It looks like we may need them."

The wolf pack harried the convoy steadily for a week, striking at dawn and at dusk each day. Nick never found out how many ships were sunk. When the attack struck against a distant segment of the big square of ships, he could not tell how many of the merchant ships went down. Within sight of the *Andrew Crichton*, eleven ships were lost.

He stood his watches four on and four off, learning to sleep fitfully in the unwieldy survival suit. He grew increasingly tired and numb, but he was dully surprised to find that he felt no conscious fear. He grew accustomed to the continuing presence of danger, and thought that it had had no effect on him until he tried, one morning, to whistle a tune with the ship's radio. He could pucker but he could not whistle.

"How long do you think they will follow us?" Nick asked the first mate one evening while he was on the wheel, after dark had fallen and the attacks for the day had ceased.

"I don't know," the first said. "Until we get air cover, I guess."

Three days out of New York, a potbellied PBY flew over

the convoy, bringing cheers from the ships as it passed over. The mate was right. There was no attack that evening.

The PBY's flew patrols over the convoy daily after that, and the wolf pack apparently turned back into the North Atlantic to find another convoy. There were no more sinkings during the last three days the convoy steamed for New York.

It was still bitterly cold, but the days were bright and clear, and after a full day without a general alarm, the crew went off double watches.

"Looks like we made it," Nick said when the first told him the deck gang would go back to four on and eight off. Both of them were still wearing the survival suits that they had lived in for a week.

"This time," the mate said dryly, "I'll be back out here in another couple of weeks, just as soon as we take on another cargo. You going to make another trip on the *Crichton?*"

"I don't know," Nick said. "I wanted to join the marines once, so I could shoot back when I'm shot at. And I'd hate to wind up like those poor bastards we left in the water."

"They shot back," the mate pointed out. "Whether they came off the destroyer or the submarine, they were shooting back when they got it."

They were silent for a few minutes, Nick busy with the wheel and the mate carefully lighting a cigarette.

"I felt the same way you do once," the mate said when he had his cigarette going. "I've been going to sea all my life, but I got the feeling when the war started that going to sea was kind of like dodging the draft. Know what I mean?"

"I know," said Nick.

"Well, it's not," the mate said. "I finally figured that they can get a lot of guys to carry a rifle. It's not that tough. But not everyone can be a mate or even a bosun or an AB. There ain't enough merchant seamen to man the ships, and there ain't enough officers, for sure. Not good ones. That's why the old man is sailing. Hell, he was retired when the war started, and he ought to be raising chickens in Iowa or someplace, like he wants to do."

"Maybe so," Nick said doubtfully. "I admit I felt like I was dodging the draft for a while, but I don't feel that way anymore. Lots of guys I know have been sitting on their butts at a desk in the army or the navy, and I've already been torpedoed twice, and we were lucky I didn't make it three on this trip. But I guess I just want to do something myself, pull a trigger or drop a bomb or something like that."

"Not me," the mate said. "I wouldn't want to be the guy who pulled the trigger that put those poor buggers in the water this trip."

"You got a point," Nick said.

The eight-to-twelve AB came in to relieve Nick, and Nick gave him the course.

"What I want to do right now," Nick told the mate, "is get this damn survival suit off. I must smell like a wet goat. A shower's going to feel good."

"That makes two of us," the mate said. "I've been itching in places I couldn't scratch for a week."

In the fo'c's'le, Nick peeled off his survival suit and the clothing under it until he was stripped. Mac came in and did the same, and Heavy, who had been on the bow and was the last to enter the fo'c's'le, was surprised when he saw them.

"You guys figure to swim ashore if we catch one?" he asked sarcastically.

"We're off double watches," Nick said. "You can take yours off, too."

"Hey, man!" Heavy said happily. "Now I can scratch my toes."

While Heavy was struggling out of his clothes, Nick and Mac paddled off to the head in their wooden shower clogs, and stayed under the weak shower for a long time, enjoying the warmth. When he had finished, Nick felt ten pounds lighter.

"I feel like I could run a mile," Mac said on the way back to the fo'c's'le. "Funny how you don't miss washing until you can't do it, and then it seems like the dirt gets two inches thick."

"Damn near was that thick," Nick said. "You want to do some laundry now?"

"You think it's safe to go below?" Mac asked.

"Sure," Nick said. "Let's get Heavy and Stringbeans and go on down."

"Heavy can't make it," Mac said. "We're still rolling too much for him to get down the ladders. We'll have to wash his clothes."

Heavy had gone to shower when they reached the fo'c's'le, so they opened his locker and gathered up his dirty clothes with their own. Stringbeans came back and looked in.

"You all doing laundry?" he asked, and Nick nodded.

"Wait up," said Stringbeans. "I'm gonna get mine. They is some dungarees I got could stand a watch all by theyselves, they is so strong."

When Stringbeans returned with his laundry bag, the three of them went down to the laundry room. They were wearing only a towel each; the laundry room, in the bowels of the ship near the engine room, was warm.

They loaded the laundry machines and sat down on a wooden bench to wait for the clothes to wash. It was hot and steamy, but the warmth felt good to Nick, and he even enjoyed sweating in the heat.

He wanted a cigarette, but he had forgotten to bring a pack, and when Mac started to light one, he borrowed a cigarette from him.

"Where did you carry them?" he asked as Mac offered him the pack.

"Tucked in the towel," Mac said.

"Got a match?"

Mac handed him the matches and shook his head. "How you fixed for spit?" he asked.

"That I got," Nick told him. "I might not have had any a couple of days ago if you had asked me then."

They smoked in silence for a few minutes.

"If we're going back down to New Orleans, we'll be breaking off from the convoy pretty soon," Nick said. "Unless we put into New York for supplies."

"Hope we don't pay off there," Stringbeans said. "Just mean I got another long trip on the train to get back to the fine ladies in New Orleans."

"If we do, we might as well sign back on the *Crichton*," Nick said. "It's a pretty good ship."

"Not me," Stringbeans said. "I'm gonna look for me a nice trip to a banana port in South America, no wolf packs around."

"Sounds good to me," Mac said.

Nick started to say that he would prefer to remain on the *Crichton*, but he was interrupted by the appearance of Heavy. The fat man was breathing heavily, and he stared around the laundry room wildly.

"What did you do with them?" he asked.

"With what?" Nick asked. Heavy was wearing a towel draped precariously around his quaking middle.

"The clothes," Heavy said. "The clothes."

"They're in the washing machine," Nick said. "Where'd you think we'd put them?"

"God-damn," Heavy said. "Stop it!"

He waddled over to the machine and stopped it and opened the door, letting a flood of water out on the deck. He scrabbled through the dripping clothes frantically while Nick and the other two watched him in amazement.

"What the hell are you doing?" Mac asked.

Heavy paid no attention. He sorted through the pile of wet clothes he had pulled out of the machine until he found a shirt tied in a knot.

Without paying any attention to Nick, Mac, and String-beans, he fumbled with the shirt until he had it open on the deck. In it were a pile of soggy pound notes and three watches, all the worse for wear.

Nick stared at the wet bills and the watches with dawning comprehension, then looked at Mac and Stringbeans.

"The dirty fat rat," Stringbeans said.

"He stole his own watches," Nick said.

Heavy looked up from counting the money and started to say something, but just then the general alarm went off. Nick froze as the alarm bell rang and rang and continued to ring until it had rung seven times. Jesus, he thought, what a time to get it! Bare-assed at the bottom of the ship, and we don't even have any clothes to put on.

He and Mac and Stringbeans had reached the foot of the ladder leading to the deck when they heard Heavy hollering behind them.

"Wait a minute!" he yelled. He was lumbering down the passageway, clutching the wet shirt to his bosom, dropping pound notes as he came.

"Shit!" Mac said. "How do we get him topside?"

"How did he get down here?" Stringbeans said unfeelingly. "If he can get below on the ladder for a few lousy bucks, he can get up on deck to save his life."

They stood and looked at Heavy, who had reached the bottom of the ladder, and stopped.

"We can't leave him," Nick said. "Put him in the middle. One guy can pull and two push."

The alarm stopped again.

"I'm all for leaving him down here," Mac said. "We'll take the pounds and leave him the watches."

Nick went first, and Heavy, surprisingly agile under the spur of fear, came second, with Mac and Stringbeans beneath him. It seemed to Nick that the trip to the main deck took hours, but it was actually only minutes before they emerged on the deck and hurried to their abandon-ship stations. Only then did Nick realize he had no clothes on.

They reached the boat deck and their lifeboat stations out of breath and shivering, and found the rest of the deck gang already at their posts. The temperature was in the vicinity of ten below; after they had been on deck for a minute, wearing nothing, Nick noticed that Heavy had begun to turn a light blue, and he knew he had, too.

"Where did they hit?" he chattered to the eight-to-twelve ordinary next to him.

"They didn't hit nowhere," the ordinary said. "Old man decided to have a fire drill."

21

Two weeks later, Nick was sitting at the bar in the Absinthe House in the French Quarter in New Orleans, waiting for Stringbeans to come in and give him a report from Curly's.

He had had two drinks and begun to worry when Stringbeans came in.

"All clear," Stringbeans said. "Curly says it's all right."

As they walked the short distance to Curly's, Nick asked Stringbeans what had delayed him.

"Man, I had to have a couple drinks," Stringbeans said.

"Was Rusty there?"

"Nope. Some other fine ladies, but not her."

Curly's Bar looked and smelled the same as it had three

months ago, when they had left New Orleans. Nick sat at the end of the bar and asked for a red-eye and drank gratefully.

Curly shambled down the bar with his stopwatch and handed it to Nick.

"Still running?" Nick asked, and Curly nodded.

Nick counted his pulse for him. It was still seventy-six.

Curly took his watch back sadly and went back down the bar and put it in the cash register. When he came back, Nick held up his empty glass, and Curly refilled it.

"Where's Rusty?" Nick asked.

"She got married," Curly said proudly. "Married a nice marine. Big man."

"That's nice," Nick said. "How come she married a marine?"

"She met him somewhere outside," Curly said. "Now she bringing him in here, and I don't like that."

"She must of swelled up pretty good by now," Stringbeans said.

"She looks a little fat," Curly said. "He don't seem to mind."

"It's a bad thing, marines coming in here," Mac said severely. "Next thing you know all the uniforms going to be coming in."

"He's the only one so far," Curly said.

"Then that must be him," Heavy said, and Nick turned around.

Rusty had come through the door, followed by a very large, strong marine with a scrambled face. He was wearing a marine dress uniform, but it did not conceal the fact that he was wide and thick and had obviously been a fighter before he had been a marine. Nick turned hastily back to the bar.

"Hi, honey," Rusty breathed in his ear, rubbing her swollen belly against his back.

"Hi," Nick said weakly, trying to pretend she was a casual acquaintance.

"Who is he?" the marine asked.

"Just an old friend," Rusty said.

"That's right," Nick said. "We were practically childhood friends."

"Childhood got something to do with it, all right," Stringbeans said.

"What's he mean?" the marine asked Rusty.

"Why don't you shut up?" Nick said to Stringbeans. "You looking for trouble?"

"You telling me to shut up?" the marine said ominously.

"No, no," Nick said. "Him."

The marine glared at Nick a moment, then took Rusty by the arm and led her to the other end of the bar, while Nick sighed with relief.

"Straight vodka," Nick said.

"You be careful," Curly told him. "Straight vodka gonna knock you, man."

"They must of fed him bananas to teach him to talk," Stringbeans said, looking at Rusty's marine. "I never see such a mean-looking man."

"Not so loud," Nick said. "He may hear you."

"You must be Nick," someone breathed in his ear. "I hear about you."

Nick turned from the bar and saw a small, dark, pneumatic young woman. She leaned on him gently.

"Who are you?" he asked.

"Mickey," she said.

"You want a brandy and sweet?"

"I'll have a Scotch instead," she told him, and Nick shook his head.

"No weak tea, baby," he said.

"Okay," she answered. "Brandy and sweet."

Curly made the brandy and sweet, and Nick made Heavy move down the bar so Mickey could sit next to him. He spent the next hour buying her brandy and sweet and improving their friendship.

He had just finished giving her an imaginative account of the dangers of the wolf packs, and decided the time had come to make his move.

"Tonight's the night," he said. "I just came back from nearly getting killed, and now I meet someone who makes it all worth while. I mean, I wonder why I'm risking my life, and then I meet you and I know. It's you."

"Oh, Nicky," she said.

"Oh, crap!" Rusty said from behind Nick. She was high, and behind her was her marine. "Don't believe his crap, honey. That's what got me this way." She patted herself on her round stomach, and Nick sighed.

"So he the one done it!" the marine said.

"She's just kidding," Nick said.

Rusty was startled to find Sam in earshot, and shook her head vigorously.

"I was just kidding," she said.

"No, you wasn't," the marine said. "Git outa the way."

"Give me a beer mug," Nick said wearily to Curly, but before Curly could comply with his request, the marine had moved Rusty out of his way with a sweep of his arm and swung at Nick.

Nick ducked under the ponderous blow and hit the marine on the chin, but with no effect. The marine's next swing missed Nick and knocked Heavy cleanly off his stool.

"Storage room," Curly said, and Nick ran down the bar and around the end of it and into the storage room, a long narrow space behind the back bar. He closed the door and leaned against one of the stacks of liquor cases lining the walls.

Through the wall he could hear vague noises from the bar, but they did not sound as if a fight were in progress. Then he heard a pounding on the door he had closed.

"He gone in there," he heard the marine say. "Clear the way. I'm gonna go right through the door."

"Get outa the way, Nick," Stringbeans hollered. "Can't stop this mother. He going through the door and me too if I don' get outa the way."

Nick backed away from the door and picked up a bottle of Scotch. He would have preferred beer on economic grounds, but he did not have time to locate a case of beer.

The door blew in and the marine came through it, and Nick hit him on the head with the bottle of Scotch. The marine staggered. Then he came on again, and Nick skipped away from him and grabbed another bottle of Scotch. When he hit the marine this time, he fell, and Nick stepped over him and walked out through the remnants of the door.

Rusty was waiting for him. She swung but missed, and Nick could guess by the weight of her bag that she had another jar of cold cream in it.

He trotted by her to the front of the bar, where Mac, Stringbeans, and Heavy were waiting.

"Let's go," he said. "We used up our welcome."

"I ain't shipping on no Liberty," Heavy told him.

"Nobody asked you," Nick said. "Let's go up to New York, coastwise. We'll ship from there."

"How come?" Mac asked.

"I don't know," Nick said. He thought about it for a minute. "Seems the nice ladies are nicer," he said, remembering Trixie. "No swingers there."